THE RESCUE
of the
Nadia Marie

David Estes

Copyright © 2021 by David Estes

All rights reserved. No part of this publication may be reproduced, distributed, or transmitted in any form or by any means, including photocopying, recording, or other electronic or mechanical methods, without the prior written permission of the publisher, except in the case brief quotations embodied in critical reviews and other noncommercial uses permitted by copyright law.

ISBN: 978-1-63945-047-3 (Paperback)
       978-1-63945-048-0 (Hardback)
       978-1-63945-049-7 (Ebook)

The views expressed in this book are solely those of the author and do not necessarily reflect the views of the publisher, and the publisher hereby disclaims any responsibility for them.

Writers' Branding
1800-608-6550
www.writersbranding.com
orders@writersbranding.com

Contents

Chapter 1	The Boat	1
Chapter 2	The Storm	20
Chapter 3	The Sheriff	25
Chapter 4	Coast Guard Honolulu	30
Chapter 5	"El Poster de los Angeles de la Estacion Militar de los Estados Unidos de Mexico."	36
Chapter 6	The Decision	38
Chapter 7	The Breakfast	40
Chapter 8	The Photo	43
Chapter 9	The Situation Room Message	45
Chapter 10	Life on the Raft	48
Chapter 11	Task Force Tango	50
Chapter 12	The Rescue Vessels	54
Chapter 13	Sara Housley	56
Chapter 14	The President	58
Chapter 15	The Situation Room	61
Chapter 16	The Reaction	64
Chapter 17	The Sighting	66
Chapter 18	The Dream	68
Chapter 19	The Breakdown	69
Chapter 20	The Cancellation	72
Chapter 21	The Pirates	73
Chapter 22	The Rendezvous	76
Chapter 23	The Fleet	81
Chapter 24	The Reckoning	83
Chapter 25	The Confirmation	88
Chapter 26	The Report	92

CHAPTER 1

The Boat

It was a dream come true for John and Julie Schwartz. The boat was the culmination of a special bond between two people that had developed over time and was rooted deep in a special love between two people. Both were avid sailors and dreamed of owning their own ocean-going sailing vessel. Julie saw an ad in a sailing magazine that listed a forty-five-foot sailing vessel for sale in Florida that seemed to fit their idea of a perfect boat. It was used but affordable and seemed to be in excellent shape. When John saw the picture of the boat, he agreed with Julie that this was the boat of their dreams. That ad started an international saga with a unique and tragic ending.

It seemed as though destiny had caused two people to come together from two different backgrounds that would merge into one special relationship.

When John was a kid, he was one of those who attracted people to him. He was fun-loving and sometimes a practical joker. When he was in grade school, he achieved the ultimate prank. He dressed up in his soldier uniform complete with gun belt, helmet, and dummy grenades. After all, it was a casual-wear day at school which coincided with Halloween. He was successful in concealing his uniform from his homeroom teacher throughout the day. When no teacher was in sight, he would display his outfit to the other kids.

It took some time before word finally reached the school principal that there was a kid running around the school in a soldier's uniform wearing grenades. The hunt was on. None of the kids would tell who it was which made the principal more determined to get to the bottom of the story. At the end of the day, John triumphantly came home with a big grin on his face. Secure in the knowledge that he had been the victor.

There was one problem. The vice principal affectionately known as Atilla, the Hundley who meted out justice with an iron hand soon found out. She liked John secretly but vowed to get even. It did not take long before Atilla, the Hundley had John in her iron grasp. He paid dearly for his indiscretion.

In high school, John became a football super jock. Of course this did have some advantages. He had no problem with the girls which drove his father crazy when these young girls started hanging around the house.

After high school, John drifted from job to job for a while. He finally ran into a friend who was working in construction. John was hired on as a laborer at his friend's construction firm.

Building things came natural to John. Since he was a child, he loved to assemble toys and design buildings. Within a couple of years, he had decided to go to college and learn how to build buildings. He graduated with honors from his engineering class.

It was not long before John had built a reputation in the trades industry. His break came when the company owner decided to retire for health reasons. John saw his opportunity to take over the business. With the assistance of one of his high school football buddies who had went into banking, he secured a loan from a bank and bought out his boss.

Within five years, John had paid off his loan early and expanded his company to become one of the largest construction firms in the State of Washington.

Through the years, John had become somewhat of a confirmed bachelor. He was happy with his life and did not seem to need to change. There were occasional girlfriends who passed through his life, but none seemed to interest him in the long term. He had no desire to live with one without being married, so he just did his thing without seeking any long-term commitment.

One night, he went to a sports bar with a couple of friends to watch a football game and just hang out. A guy named Jason, who

John knew but did not like very well, came into the bar with a girl who worked with him. John seemed oddly curious as to who she was.

When Jason went to use the restroom, John saw his chance. He went over to the girl and asked her how well she knew Jason. To his surprise, he found that she had literally met him at the door. They both worked together, and she had decided to keep Jason company while she waited for a girlfriend to show up.

John was immediately attracted to this girl and wanted to get to know her. He found out that her name was Julie. She was a manager of a high-end car dealership in Bellevue, Washington.

John felt that this girl was too intelligent to be running around with someone like Jason. He would have to fix that minor problem. Without hesitation, he gave Julie his business card and asked her to call him later in the week. Julie, after some charm and coaxing, finally agreed to at least call. She too had become curious about this rather straightforward stranger. She made a note to ask about him before she would call.

Julie had grown up on a farm near Seattle. She had attended schools in the Seattle area. During her early years, Julie had girlfriends whom she was completely satisfied to associate with. Boys were not on her list of things to really pay much attention to.

She too excelled at sports. Julie was a top-class runner who took numerous first place prizes at her school track meets. Julie had early on decided that she would be successful in life and would not depend on anyone for her support. In high school, she more often than not eschewed school drinking parties.

One time, she gave in to her girlfriend's pestering to go to a party. It got raided by the police. She had to endure the shame of having her parents come to the police station and escorting her home. Julie vowed to never do anything like that again.

College was easy for her. She had to get a part-time job to help pay her expenses, but the job did not interfere with her studies or her grades. She graduated with top honors. While in college, Julie majored in business administration and economics. When she graduated, Julie found a couple of jobs in fields that she did not like. Ironically, she was asked to manage a car dealership that was having financial trouble. She did not know anything about cars and had no desire to learn. However, one of her friends from high school was on the board of directors and asked her to come and assist in turning the company around.

Her new job was not an easy task. Her good friend had failed to tell Julie that the company was run by the son of the original owner. This individual was your basic coke user and drunk. Julie had no tolerance of him.

Within a matter of weeks, Julie had a confrontation with the father who was the chairman of the board and semi-retired. Julie let him know in no uncertain terms that his son would be the downfall of the company if he was left to manage it. She told the old man that she did not need this job and intended to move on with her life.

No one had dared to speak to the old man like she did. Everyone was expecting an immediate dismissal. To their surprise, the old man began to listen to Julie as she laid out each and every bad decision the son had made. She even included the son's drug use and heavy drinking; all taboo subjects in the company.

After giving her presentation, Julie handed the old man her two-week notice and walked out of the room. To her surprise, she received a memo from the old man stating that she was the new chief executive officer effectively immediately. His son was to remain on the board of directors but would take no part in the operation of the business. Shortly after, the son checked into rehab. He never returned to the company.

Julie was prevailed upon by members of the board and friends she had made after coming there to take the position. Reluctantly she agreed. Within months, Julie had the business turned around and making a profit. She bought out the son's share of stocks and became a minor stockholder. When other members of the board left or retired, she bought them out as well. Within a short period of time, she was a full partner in the company.

There was one individual on the board of directors of the company who was also a stockholder that drove Julie crazy. His name was Jack Ryan whom Julie called Jack Ass Ryan. Jack Ass was constantly criticizing Julie and making life miserable for her in general.

Julie would dream of ways to get even with this Neanderthal jerk, such as the Chinese water torture, bamboo shoots under his fingernails, a firing squad, or just plain cutting his balls off.

Unexpectedly, Julie prevailed. She came to work one day to find a letter on her desk from Jack Ass. The letter read that Jack Ass had decided to sell his shares in the company and resign his board position. It turned out that Jack Ass had been taking his stress from a failed marriage out on Julie every chance he got. His wife Marlene solved the problem for Julie. She took Jack Ass to the cleaners in the divorce settlement.

Julie was home celebrating her victory when she saw the boat ad in the magazine.

When Julie first encountered John, her reaction to John was one of bemused interest. He was somewhat aggressive and a little arrogant yet he had a likeable quality about him that interested her.

Through the years, Julie had met various men that she felt would make a good companion. As she got to know each of them, she found some glaring fault or just a lack of compatibility. Some she became friends with on a platonic level. One she did have some strong feelings for but discovered he was married. From that time on, she was very cautious whom she let into her inner feelings. Mainly, she stuck with girlfriends. They were safer emotionally.

To Julie's surprise, John came by the dealership a couple of days later and asked to buy a new SUV. Julie saw him there by accident and greeted him warmly as she did all potential customers. She had already learned from mutual friends that John was a long-time bachelor who owned a construction firm. It was rumored that he was quite wealthy but seemed to be more down to earth than most. If he had wealth, he hid it quite well. If asked what he did for a living, John would reply that he was a construction worker.

John had done some research himself. He learned that Julie was a managing partner of her company. She was viewed as somewhat standoffish toward guys but had a good sense of humor and was pleasant to talk to. Julie, it appeared, was a person who would take charge and make it plain that she would handle any situation when others failed. To the guys, she was good-looking and a real babe.

Julie and John struck up a conversation at the dealership that day that went from a hello to lunch and a promise to get together for a musical presentation at the local opera house in Seattle. It wasn't long before they became inseparable. Within a year, they were married.

John was an avid sailor. He had a small sailboat that he puttered around Puget Sound on. He dreamed of owning a large sailboat and taking it on a cruise to Hawaii or just about any place he could safely go to in a small sailing vessel.

Once he married Julie, the two of them became sailing partners. They sailed all over the Puget Sound area fishing and skin diving or just hanging out on the boat with friends.

It wasn't long before their utopia came to an end. Julie became pregnant. It was to be a girl according to the doctor. Both agreed to name her Nadia Marie. The child was darling. John would toss her around like a rag doll just to hear her laugh and coo. Julie frowned on the rough housing like any mother, but she would take it in stride and smiled inwardly watching John and baby Nadia play.

As Nadia grew, her personality began to come through. She had an angelic smile that would turn any heart from the day she was born. When she was up to something and got caught, she had a sneaky smile that betrayed her. She was incapable of telling a lie. Nadia was a parent's dream. She seldom complained and was obedient to a fault. As she grew, her parents' pride in her grew.

There was one sadness in Nadia's life. Her parents worked during the day, and she had a nanny. The nanny was named Cathy. Cathy was okay and lots of fun, but she could not take the place of her father and mother. Nadia would sometimes count the hours to when her parents would come home.

Sometimes, Nadia would play a pretend game. She would watch out the window and pretend that Mommy and Daddy were in a race to come home. She dreamed that there were floods, fire, and earthquakes that kept her parents away. They would overcome all these obstacles to reach home. The first parent to arrive would be the winner of a huge hug each day. Nadia couldn't wait for the weekend when she would have her parents to herself for two whole days.

Sailing was fun for Nadia. At an early age, she learned to help with the boat. By the time she was nine, she understood the workings of a sailing craft. She even understood the sailing lingo.

What was more fun was to sit on the prow of the boat and pretend that she was a pirate searching out treasure ships to attack. Sometimes she was a princess and waited for her prince to come and rescue her from the pirates.

One day, John was sitting on a boat with a few of his buddies drinking and hanging out while talking about the good and bad times they had. One of them was kidding him about sneaking in on Jason and stealing his girlfriend while he was in the bathroom. All got a chuckle out of it.

One friend suggested to John that he should run for political office. John's reaction was to laugh. A couple of other friends chimed in and told John he would make a good politician.

Just to gain the high road in the conversation, John half-jokingly told the group that if they were so serious about the election, then all they had to do was cough up money for a campaign. He thought that comment would put the whole thing to rest.

A couple of days later, two of his buddies walked into his office with sly grins on their faces. John thought, "What are these two turkeys up to? Shouldn't they be at work?"

To his surprise, he was told by one of his friends named Dave that the group had some dinner and drinks at a local watering hole and decided that he should run for political office. Pledges were made for money, and some volunteered to take certain positions in the campaign.

John's initial reaction was to throw these two out of his office for being clowns and wasting his time. The only trouble was they looked serious. These two had not been serious in their whole lives. When John realized what was being said, he stopped to think about it. He told the two that he would think about it and get back to them.

After his friends left, John stopped what he was doing to mull over what he had been told. In the end, he decided he should give back to the community that had given him so much. He decided to run for the state legislature.

That night at dinner, he told Julie about his friends' visit. John told Julie that he felt that he could give back to the community. Julie's position was that John must not let this new adventure interfere with their homelife. When Nadia heard the news, she just let out a deep breath and rolled her eyes.

John was undaunted. He and his friends set up a small campaign headquarters in one of his buildings and started campaigning. To his surprise, he won.

Julie was lukewarm to the idea at first but soon got into the swing of things and helped out. She helped John because he did feel that he was contributing and had his heart set on serving others. It was important to John. That was all that counted.

Julie wasn't so open with her giving. She would listen at work or at church to see if anyone had a hardship worth helping with. If she found a deserving person or family, she would find a way to help them anonymously. One time, she paid for an operation for one of her workers children. She had a trusted friend make the donation so that no one would ever find out.

Another time, Julie was out walking with Nadia. She came across a coworker's home who had a large family. She stopped to chat with his wife. The wife told Julie that the family car was broken down with a tune-up problem. They did not have the money to fix the car. Julie had a money order sent to the family and marked it "car repair."

A couple of weeks later, Julie came walking by the home and saw the wife again. She and Julie exchanged pleasantries. The wife told her a story about getting a money order in the mail that had no signature. It had "car repair" marked on it. The wife felt that an aunt had done it even though the aunt denied it. After a brief conversation, Julie went on with Nadia to finish their walk. She had a small smile on her face. She just did not want solicitors around her like dogs in heat every day. It was enough satisfaction to see the appreciation the woman had stated to her.

Julie was the pragmatic one of the family. She would shop at secondhand stores instead of going to the fancy downtown stores. When John decided to find a large sailing craft to take on an extended cruise, she insisted they buy a used boat.

Julie was home and celebrating her victory over Jack Ass Ryan and just being lazy. Nadia was in school, and the nanny was out shopping. Julie was reading a boat magazine on the couch when she came across an ad for a used forty-five-foot sailing boat. Instantly, she felt that this was *the* boat.

When she showed the boat to John, he liked it. They agreed that this was a good opportunity to take some time off. The boat was in Florida. They could fly down to Orlando and visit the Epcot Center with Nadia. From there, they would go buy the boat and set sail for Hawaii through the Panama Canal then back to Seattle. Their journey would take about a month and a half.

Julie became the chief negotiator for the boat. She called up the broker and asked why the boat was being sold. She was told that an older couple had bought the boat new with the intent of sailing around the horn and going to the Polynesian Islands in the Pacific. Their plans were dashed when the husband contracted cancer. His fight for his life, though valiant, had ended in his death after many months. The wife lost interest in the boat and was selling it.

The boat had seen some use for a couple of years before the owner got sick. After his death, the boat was put into dry dock storage where it was waiting to be sold. Julie had the broker take various pictures and send them to her. She drove the broker nuts with all her requests. Finally, she was satisfied and made an offer. Much to her surprise, the offer was accepted immediately.

If the boat stood up to her inspection on arrival in Florida, she informed the broker, her and her husband intended to buy it. A date was set for them to come and inspect the boat.

Nadia was ecstatic when she heard the news. She bounced around the house like Tigger singing, "Yah! We're going on a boat ride! Yah! Yah!" She was as happy as a little—well, almost eleven—eleven-year-old girl could be. Cathy, the nanny, threatened to hog-tie her to a chair if she did not settle down.

Nadia got on the phone and called all her girlfriends to let them know that she was going on a trip with her parents. She most certainly had to tell them she was going on a sailboat. The whole adventure would take all of the summer.

Nadia called her best friend Sara to give her a detailed description of her preparations for the trip every day. There were decisions that had to be made. Should she forego clothes and take toys instead. The biggest decision was which doll she would take Samantha or Josephina. Sara wasn't much help. She just sighed and told Nadia to leave them all home. Nadia chose to take them all. That way, none would have their feelings hurt. Cathy put a stop to it when she saw a suitcase full of dolls and no clothes or underwear.

Nadia tried to appeal to her mother to no avail. She finally reconciled herself to taking Samantha, Josephina, and baby blanket. Thanks to that old meanie head Cathy.

The plane ride was in itself exciting. She got to sit by a window and look out at the world as it went passing by. There were the mountains and then the plains as far as the eye could see. People and cars looked like small ants.

When they got to the Epcot Center, Nadia was awed by the rides and fairy-tale characters. She loved the Maelstrom with its polar bears, Viking ship, and Pirates. The monorail was fun to ride as you went to each event.

Nadia was fascinated with the various pavilions. There was a German pavilion, an Italian pavilion, a Mexican pavilion, and a Japanese pavilion. Each of the sites had presentations in the native language. Languages fascinated Nadia. She loved to listen to the various voice inflections of each language. The German language sounded like someone who had had too much beer to drink. Most of the other languages were spoken too fast. When the speaker slowed down, Nadia could pick up on the rhythm of the language.

The beach was okay, but Nadia liked the pool at the World Dolphin Hotel. She could sit on the side of the pool or swim. No one tried to step over her or kick sand on her. Besides, she imagined that there were sharks in the ocean, and she did not like the thought of a shark eating her.

Finally, they left fairy-tale land and went to get their boat. The boat itself was a beautiful boat. The masts were so tall that Nadia could hardly see to the top. She thought that a pirate could sit up on top and see the whole world.

Inside the boat, Nadia had her own bunk area which became her palace. She would pretend that she was a princess and her pirate prince would come and take her away to an enchanted land of fairies, unicorns, and dragons.

Of course, the boat had a tape player. When Nadia was not helping her parents sail the boat, she would read books or watch such movies as *The Goonies*, *Hannah Montana*, *iCarly*, and *Suite Life on Deck*. Nadia would pretend that she was on a cruise ship with the characters from the show *Suite Life on Deck*. She liked the character London because she was cool and filthy rich. The second best character she liked was One Eye Willie from *The Goonies*. He was scary.

The best part though was that she was with both her parents.

She liked to help with the boat. Just helping and having her parents to herself was all she cared about. Her chest really puffed up when her parents named the boat the *Nadia Marie*.

Once they set sail, their route took them around the Florida Peninsula bypassing the Keys and on by New Orleans to Corpus Christi Texas. Going through the Gulf of Mexico was awesome. Nadia was awestruck by the huge oil rigs and gigantic oil tankers that plied through the gulf.

Near Corpus Christi, Nadia had a couple of thrilling experiences with a boat in distress and the United States Coast Guard.

Traveling along the Texas coastline close to a place called San Jose Island near Corpus Christi, Nadia's parents heard a distress signal over the emergency frequency on their radio. Their GPS indicated that the boat was about five nautical miles from their position. Nadia's father altered his course and headed toward the boat in distress.

Aboard the boat, which was a sailing boat like theirs, there was a family of four. John threw the boat a line and towed them into Corpus Christi. Shortly after leaving a grateful family behind, and on the way past Brownsville, Texas, Nadia saw a large boat in the distance moving fast toward their position. When the boat neared, she could see the big stripe and a flag of a United States Coast Guard cutter.

Nadia could hear on the radio that the cutter was directing her father to lower his sails and prepare to be boarded. "Boy," thought

Nadia, "this is just like in the movies with pirates being chased by the good guys."

Soon a small boat detached itself from the larger boat and came along their boat. A sailor in a white uniform came aboard and talked to John and Julie while Nadia watched. After a short conversation, the sailor got back into his small boat and returned to the larger boat.

After the sailor left, Nadia asked her dad what the man wanted. John replied teasingly, "The man was looking for pirates. He thought you were a pirate, but we convinced him that you were our daughter. He wanted to take you to pirate jail."

Nadia replied, "You are teasing, Daddy!"

John went on to explain, "Honey, there are bad people in the world. Some of them use boats to carry out their crimes. It is the job of the Coast Guard to catch them so they will not hurt little girls like you, or hurt Mommy and I. They keep us safe and help us when we need help like that family we helped."

Nadia couldn't wait to tell her friends about the encounter. She thought it was exciting. Once they were across the international boundary into Mexico, John chose to stop at Veracruz to sign in with Mexican Customs known as Aduanas. Their route was to take them to Cancun before setting sail for the Panama Canal Zone.

At Veracruz, John did not want to stay for any length of time. There had been trouble with Mexican drug gangs, and he did not want to encounter any trouble. There was a short visit to Castillo De San Juan De Ulua, the old Veracruz fort, on Callega Island, then around the Yucatan Peninsula to Cancun.

Cancun was not much better. There had been drug gang violence in the city. As a result of the violence, the United States Embassy had issued a travel advisory.

After taking on supplies at Cancun, John, Julie, and Nadia left for the Costa Rican Port of Limon. There they decided to take a short respite and spend a day at the Tortuguero National Park. The green turtles were coming in for their annual egg-laying on the beaches. A guided tour bus took them up and back to their boat.

The Rescue of the Nadia Marie

There wasn't a great deal to see in Puerto Limon. Tourists did stop in occasionally, but for the most part, Puerto Limon was a working port that exported a lot of bananas.

The next stop was Panama. That was to be a challenge. Small boats are not allowed to transverse the Panama Canal alone. It is cost prohibitive and a waste of time. In order for a small boat to go through the canal, it must go with a group of small boats. To get through the morass of bureaucratic rules and regulations governing the Canal Zone, it was easier to hire an agent whose job it is to see that you get through the canal and all paperwork is filed.

John had used the Internet to find an agent while they were in Miami. He had the unlikely name of Hans Soleto. Hans had been recommended by another boater they met casually in Miami. John wondered where a Panamanian got a German name, but he did not want to know and wasn't going to ask.

As the *Nadia Marie* neared the Canal area, John contacted Hans by calling a prearranged number. Hans instructed John to proceed to the Shelter Bay Marina. There, Hans was waiting to take John to the Port Captain's Office. Hans had the basic yacht arrival documents filled out. John had faxed him the basic information on the boat and the personal information on Julie, Nadia, and himself.

John had arrived on one of those days when a representative from the Port Captain's Office was where he could be reached easily. His name was Juan which is Spanish for John.

Juan did not particularly like Norte Americanos. He found many of them rude, obnoxious, and arrogant. He took great delight in making life miserable for them. Hans, of course, knew this and usually went along with Juan when one of the arrogant ones was encountered.

Juan's favorite approach was to feign ignorance of English when he wanted to teach someone a lesson. In this case, Juan took a liking to this Americano. He seemed pleasant and cooperative. His wife was "muy bonita" and so was his little girl. Juan decided to not take up a lot of time with this family. Besides, he had a "muy bonita senorita" he was going out to dinner with and needed to go shopping for a present for her.

Hans and Juan conferred for a brief time, then Juan signed all the necessary paperwork and left. Hans then took John, Julie, and Nadia to a small café to talk to them. Hans explained that one of the rules governing the canal is that each boat had to have at least five passengers. Hans kept a list of travelers that wanted to hitch a ride through the canal. These travelers were usually college students traveling for fun and the experience. Hans had the names of a couple of young women who were waiting for the right boat to come through so they could go through the locks and get to the Pacific side of the canal. Hans told John and Julie that he would contact the women and let them know that they could go through with the *Nadia Marie.*

Their departure date and time was set for two days away. This gave John and Julie time to take Nadia shopping. Hans made arrangements for them to rent a car to take to Colon where they could buy presents to send home and food for the boat. There was a fairly large supermarket in Cuatro Altos known as the Rey supermarket.

John was able to pick up a few tools at a place called Novey's in the Millenium Plaza near Cuatro Altos. John had wanted to pick up a couple of Marine Batteries. He felt that the present batteries on the boat were older and might need replacing. He made a mental note to find a place to buy them back at the marina.

Nadia was having so much fun shopping that John forgot about the batteries and concentrated on having fun with Julie and Nadia. By the end of the day, all of them were tired, and all shopped out. They returned to the Shelter Bay Marina tired but happy.

Dinner was an extra bonus. John ate a huge steak. Julie gorged herself on seafood. Nadia just had fish and chips. She did not like the expensive stuff and decided to stick with the kid food.

The next day was hectic. John had to talk to the other boat owners and Hans about the transit through the canal. The *Nadia Marie* would be included in a group of yachts along with a large tanker named the John T. Marsten registered out of Liberia and owned by a shipping firm from Ireland.

Hans had delivered 125-foot ropes to the boats to ensure that they would stick together. It had been decided that the boats would go in sets of threes. Their time for departure was set for 1400 hours the following afternoon.

Later in the day, Hans came aboard with two female passengers. It turned out they were two students from the University of Washington in Seattle. They were sisters named Joyce and Anna Hansen. Both were pleasant and willing to help with the departure.

Joyce helped Julie stow the food and gear. Anna took a liking to Nadia and took care of her while the others had to run errands and check out of the marina. Finally, the day for departure arrived. All boats proceeded to an area off the Port of Cristobal known as the flats. There, they met an advisor who would escort them through the locks.

Once they ascended through the Gatun Locks, the boats anchored in Gatun Lake. The following day, the boats finished the transit through the canal. They arrived at the Flamenco Marina the following afternoon.

Panama requires anyone staying in country for more than three days to apply for a visa. John and Julie decided that it was not worth staying and having to go through the paperwork hassle. They dropped off the Hansen sisters, then set sail for the open ocean.

Nadia was saddened by the departure of Anna Hansen. They had become good friends. Anna was the younger of the two sisters. She was a freshman at the University of Washington. Joyce, Anna's elder sister, was going to be a senior. Anna was majoring in psychology but had a minor in languages. Nadia told her how she too was interested in languages. Anna took Nadia to one of the sidewalk cafés near the marina. They sat and listened to people from all over the world speak in their native tongues. Anna would tell Nadia what language was being spoken. Sometimes, Anna would let Nadia try to guess the language. It was fun.

Nadia had acquired an interest in other languages ever since her teacher had the students in her class listen to foreign languages on a tape recorder. Here, she could listen to real live people talk. She would miss Anna.

Their route took them up the coastline north. Sometimes Nadia would lean over the railing and look at the ocean. Sometimes the ocean turned into a sea of glass. During that time, the ocean would be a beautiful deep blue. Other times, the ocean would turn aqua. Her dad said the color of the ocean was merely a reflection of the cloud colors.

Once they had spotted a pod of whales. Another time, as they came close to land, a group of dolphins followed them for almost half a day. It was exciting to Nadia.

Their route took them from the canal to Acapulco which was the first stop on the way north to Ensenada, Mexico. Acapulco was filling up with college students, so John and Julie decided to continue on to Puerto Vallarta. At Puerto Vallarta, the crowds were getting as bad as Acapulco.

At Mazatlan, the crowds were a little more mature and tolerable. The *Nadia Marie* and company decided to lay over for a short rest at a local hotel. Mazatlan was fun for Nadia. She got to go on a short tour to two old Mexican towns called Copaca and Concordia. On Stone Island, she got to go horseback riding.

After a couple of days of sightseeing, they left for Cabo San Lucas. Cabo was filled with college students as well. John almost got into a fight with a drunken student at a restaurant. John decided it was best to cut their stay short and head for their final stop at Ensenada, Mexico.

En route to Ensenada, they encountered a sad but too often problem on the ocean. One day, Nadia was watching for whales through her dad's binoculars when she saw a small whale circling a much bigger orca whale that seemed to be floating on the surface of the water and not moving. Nadia called to her parents and pointed to the whale. "Look," she said, "that whale is in trouble or dying!"

John took the binoculars and looked in the direction that Nadia was pointing. "The whale is alive. I see its tail moving, but it can't seem to right itself. We will take a closer look and see what is wrong." Julie who had been at the helm changed course and set sail for a course that would bring them parallel to the whale, but a safe distance away. Once they got near to the whale, Julie and John lowered the sails to cut their speed.

John took the binoculars and scanned the whale once again. The smaller whale had moved closer to the larger whale and was emitting a shrill sound. John slowly lowered the binoculars. His face had turned beet red. Nadia knew her father was angry. He slowly turned and looked at Nadia then at Julie. "That whale is caught in a fishnet! It will die if something is not done. There is no one but us in the area that can help. I guess it is up to us to do something."

A simple plan was devised. Julie would maneuver the sailboat close but a safe distance from the whale. John would take the small skiff and approach the whale. If the whale did not panic, John would attempt to cut the net from the whale. Julie put out a general call for assistance over the international frequency. A nearby marine biology vessel picked up the call and responded. Their ETA was about four hours.

John got into the skiff and motored over to the whale. The whale lay on its side and seemed to be breathing heavily. John could see the whale's eyes following him as he approached. At first, the whale seemed to be trying to get away from John but settled down as John talked to it. It seemed to sense that John was there to help. The smaller whale moved off a short distance and waited and watched.

On close inspection, John could see that the whale's blowhole was partially blocked by the fishnet. The first order of business was to free the blowhole so the whale could breathe better.

To accomplish the task, John only had a filleting knife. The net was thicker than he originally thought. It appeared that the whale had encountered the net. In a panic to rid itself of the net, the whale began to thrash about. That only caused the net to become more entangled, eventually wrapping itself around the whale. The net itself had small metal cords interwoven in the net to give it strength. Luckily, John had brought a pair of cable snips with him. He would first cut the synthetic rope, then the cable strings. The task was slow and tedious. It took over an hour to clear the net from the whale's blowhole.

Once the whale was free to breathe, it suddenly sank and then came to the surface and blew water all over John. John had to time his work with the whale's breathing. It was obvious to John and Julie that the whale knew that John was trying to free her. The whale remained still while John cut away the net. Some progress was being made. Occasionally, John had to stop to sharpen his knives that were dulled by the thin steel cable intertwined in the net.

John was not much of an environmentalist. As he worked and sweated removing the net, he asked himself over and over again why he was doing this. He didn't have a real high opinion of tree huggers and Greenpeace types. In spite of his personal beliefs, he kept at the net. His arms ached, and his back hurt, but he kept going. A quiet determination had set upon him, and he was determined to set this whale free. Besides, what would he tell Nadia if he gave up?

About three and a half hours into the effort, Nadia excitedly reported that a boat was approaching from the west. The marine biology boat was arriving. Once the marine biology crew arrived, they took over the operation. John was exhausted and glad to let them take over. Divers were sent to look at the net underneath the whale's belly. Heavy-duty cutting equipment was deployed and set to work cutting the net. Within a couple of hours, the net fell away, and the whale was freed.

As the whale moved away to the open ocean, cheers and shouts went up from the two groups. Nadia started dancing around and yelling, "Yah! Yah!" Handshakes were exchanged and backs were slapped, then the *Nadia Marie* pulled away and headed for Ensenada. About half a day out of Ensenada, Nadia was the first to notice. A pod of killer whales were approaching the boat. They soon encircled the boat and seemed to be escorting it across the ocean—a simple tribute to someone who had helped one of their own. A few miles out of Ensenada, the pod disappeared.

Ensenada was an important jumping-off point. It was over two thousand nautical miles from Ensenada to Hawaii. The boat had to be checked and rechecked. Sails were inspected. Extra line was bought in case a line broke. John had the boat hauled out of the water, and the hull inspected for any cracks or damage. Food was secured and stowed. John made sure there was extra food and water. Oil was changed in the engines, and a compression test was made to be sure all was in working order. John thought he had told the boatyard to install two new marine batteries to the bilge pumps. The serviceman overlooked the batteries, and John was too busy to check to see if they had been installed.

Julie and Nadia, in the meantime, went shopping. As they bought presents, usually shoes and clothing, they would pack them up and send them home for Cathy to store until they got home. Of course, there were things for Cathy as well. Julie did not want to leave her out.

After all, she had to stay behind and take care of the house while the family was away. Julie made a mental note to buy Cathy a vacation package to Hawaii for her help.

On arrival at Ensenada, John checked in with the local Aduanas or customs. He filed a sailing plan with them just in case. It was an easy thing to do since the Coral Hotel and Marina, where they were staying, had a local Aduana office and staff.

Julie and Nadia found an Internet room at the hotel and sent e-mails to friends and relatives updating them on their progress. Cathy was e-mailed their sailing plans listing the date of departure and approximate date of arrival in Hawaii.

After a short stay, they set sail for the trip to Hawaii.

CHAPTER 2

The Storm

As the boat left the harbor at Ensenada, the sun was just rising. There was a slight cloud haze that caused the sun to reflect a golden glow that turned into a kaleidoscope of colors. Nadia was awestruck by the beauty.

As the days began to pass on the open ocean, the family began to settle in to a routine. John and Julie took care of the sails. Both would stand watch at the helm. Sometimes Nadia was allowed to stand watch for short periods at the helm to teach her how to steer the boat.

Nadia's job was to check the food and water supply and make sure food was ready to be prepared for meals. She was tasked with making the beds and changing the bedding as needed. Swabbing the deck was not her favorite, but she took on the task and got the job done. Sometimes her mother would help her with her chores. It was great doing things with her parents. She was happy with the voyage and time spent with her parents.

It wasn't a big storm as storms go. It came up just as dawn was breaking. The wind began to pick up and then the sky clouded up. There were some swells but nothing the boat could not handle. It was a seagoing vessel and could withstand fairly large swells.

Sometimes when accidents happen, it is not a single cause. There are a number of errors that occur that when added together, eventually cause the accident. Such was the case with the *Nadia Marie*.

Normally, two people can handle a forty-foot vessel. With Nadia aboard, the task was made easier because she could help with the non-critical tasks that needed to be handled on a daily basis. In this case, the normal turned into the critical.

When the wind became too strong, John and Julie lowered the sails, which was standard procedure. John tied off the mast in a hurry. He failed to check the lines to make sure they were secure enough. He did not discover that he had failed to tie the rope tight.

In Florida, John had discovered that the battery gauge showed that the batteries were low. He did not pay much attention to it since they would charge once the engine was started and they were underway. He had misread the gauges.

The gauge was not only showing that the batteries were low but that they were not holding a charge properly. They were old batteries that needed replacing. Once underway, the batteries charged up, and John did not pay much attention. He did notice that the bilge pumps seemed to run the batteries down fairly quickly when they were at full sail without the engine running. John would simply start the engine and charge them back up. He made a mental note to buy new ones when he got to where he could have the boat serviced. It was a fatal error for the *Nadia Marie*.

Everything was running smoothly. John and Julie had secured the hatches and sails for inclement weather. The *Nadia Marie* easily encountered and attacked each wave as it broke against the bow of the vessel. John, Julie, and Nadia were enjoying a cup of hot chocolate when the engine failed. John went to check on the engine while Julie steered the boat.

Unknown to John, the previous owner had been using gasoline that contained ethanol. It wasn't the owner's fault. The marina owner where the *Nadia Marie* was moored had decided to cut cost and bought the gasoline with ethanol in it. He did not tell the boat owners about his use of gasoline mixed with ethanol. Ethanol will eventually clog up the carburetor on boats that use it. At this critical time, the fuel system failed causing the *Nadia Marie's* engine to quit.

Diagnosing the engine problem did not take long. John quickly determined that there was something wrong with the fuel system. Luckily, he had brought along tools and replacement parts just in case. He estimated it would take about two hours to fix the problem. The carburetor would have to be taken out and cleaned and the fuel filter replaced. Just as John started into the engine compartment with his tools, he was suddenly and violently thrown against the bulkhead. The boat seemed to spin and tilt at the same time. Julie called out, "John, come up here!" John made his way topside to find out what had happened. Julie was straining to turn the boat into the wind. The main sail mast boom had slipped one of its tie downs and was swaying back and forth. Luckily, the second tie down had held but was loose and slipping. It would be a matter of time before the boom came loose entirely and would have swung over the side of the boat which would have been disastrous.

John went to secure the loose tie down. His timing was not very good. Just as he reached for the loose rope, the boat tilted and then swung back unexpectedly. The mast boom struck John, knocking him unconscious. Julie saw the boom just as it swung back. She tried to warn John, but it was too late. When John went down, Julie called to Nadia, "Nadia, hand me that small rope."

Nadia quickly handed her mother the rope. Julie took the rope and tied off the helm.

"Nadia, take hold of the helm."

"Got it, Mom," said Nadia.

"Now hold the helm as steady as you can while I go help your father."

Julie grabbed a first aid kit and hurried outside. Nadia did the best she could to hold the helm steady.

Once outside, Julie could see that John was bleeding from a nasty gash to his forehead. She quickly put a bandage on his head to stop the bleeding. John was breathing okay but was still unconscious and moaning. Once John was taken care of, Julie quickly set about securing the mast boom. Once the boom was secure, she returned to the cabin to check on Nadia. Nadia was struggling but had kept the boat on course.

"Hang in there a little longer, sweetheart," Julie said. "I need to get Daddy inside, then I can help you."

Julie returned to the deck. John was still not fully conscious but had begun to come to. Julie helped him inside the cabin and put him on a couch. Julie, with the help of Nadia, divided her time between steering the boat and tending to John who was still not fully conscious enough to be of help.

The sea calmed for a short period which allowed Julie to take stock of the situation and form a plan. Her first priority was to see that the boat was stable. Then she would have to tend to John and try to get him awake enough to help Nadia steer the boat while she looked at the engine. Her efforts were thwarted by John's condition. When he attempted to stand, he would become dizzy and begin to pass out. Julie's focus began to be on John and steering the boat.

Once again, the wind came up, and the ocean swells increased. Julie had to turn her attention to the boat. Nadia did what she could to tend to her father. It took awhile before Julie noticed that the boat was lower in the water and seemed to be slow in responding to the helm. She noticed too that the waves were washing across the bow, and the water was dripping into the downstairs area. When she went to check the downstairs, her worst fears were realized. The bilge pumps had quit, and there was water on the floor. Julie could not manually pump and steer the boat at the same time. She realized that the boat was going to sink.

"Stop and think! Stop and think!" was going through Julie's mind. "Don't panic, remain calm." She had to think. First, she would send out a distress signal, then prepare the lifeboat in case the boat sank and a rescue was not close. Julie returned to the cabin and went to the marine radio. She tuned to the emergency frequency and began to broadcast.

"This is the *Nadia Marie*, Mayday! Mayday! We are sinking and need immediate help. Can anyone hear this transmission? Please respond." She repeated the message several times with no response. Finally, Julie gave up and began to make preparations for launching the life raft. She had Nadia find all the water bottles and food she could quickly grab. All the provisions and emergency signals were placed into the life raft. A small tarp was put in to keep them from the sun if they were not found right away. Julie hoped that someone had heard her call for assistance and would attempt a rescue. She was planning for the worst-case scenario, however.

The storm seemed to increase which accelerated the water flow into the boat. Julie decided that it was best to launch the life raft in the storm and not remain in the boat. She helped John and Nadia onto the deck and pushed the raft off the side of the boat. Then she had Nadia and John get in while she untied the raft from the boat. Helping John into the raft was a chore but all went fairly well and soon everyone was in the raft and secure. As the raft drifted away from the boat, the boat turned broadside to the wind, then slowly tipped on its side.

CHAPTER 3

The Sheriff

It had been a tough six months for Sheriff Eldon Fogus. He had almost been beaten for reelection. Then a deputy had been caught stealing. His wife died, and a deputy was shot and killed. He needed a vacation!

Cops are human even though they do not show outward emotion. If you become emotional in the cop world, you lose control of the situation. That could spell disaster. Cops suppress their emotions and feelings to the point that they appear to become unfeeling and disconnected from reality around them. Yet underneath that stern outward appearance, human misery takes its toll, especially if a personal tragedy happens to them.

Over a period of years, cops become stressed out. Almost all of them hide their stress or deal with it in different ways. Some become withdrawn. Some drink. Some have affairs and voice their frustrations to their "chippies" which is police talk for a mistress. In the end, the "chippie" becomes stressed and breaks off the relationship. Most often, the wife finds out and there is a divorce. Too often, cops care too much and the job destroys them. Sometimes the job becomes their life, and when they retire, their life is over. When it is time to retire, the cop just puts his gun barrel in his mouth and pulls the trigger. Most build a family relationship that is a buffer between them and the job. Those kinds of cops make it through life and on to retirement.

Eldon Fogus missed his wife terribly. Cancer had struck suddenly and without warning. One month, she was vibrant and alive. The next month, she was dead. She had been his support and partner for thirty-five years. They had gone to high school together and had been a part of each other's life all their adult lives. They had three wonderful children who had gone on to college and had outstanding careers.

Eldon was now alone and the stress of the job and the loneliness of the loss of his wife had almost overwhelmed him. He was going to lie on a beach and relax for the first time in his life. Besides, he simply wanted to be left alone.

Sheriff Fogus had booked a flight for the South Pacific and intended to get away from his stressful circumstance. The Australian Outback was calling his name, and he intended to go there. First, he would stop in Hawaii and go hiking to see the volcanos, then he would head out for the Outback.

One of the characteristics of a person under stress is that they will just stare aimlessly. It is not important what they stare at. They just check out mentally and go off into a mental oblivion. Eldon had lapsed into a mental state of oblivion and was just staring out the window of the plane at the ocean below. The sun was about to come up and was starting to reflect off the ocean. He was watching the sun glare as it moved with the plane. Nothing in particular was going through his mind.

Police officers are trained to look for something that does not belong or something that is out of place with the surroundings. As Eldon stared out the window, something began to seep into his subconscious. There was a tiny pinpoint of light that was not moving with the glare of the morning sun as the plane moved through the air. The tiny pinpoint of light was flashing off and on. Eldon fixed on the light and began to stare at it. He suddenly realized that the light was flashing the SOS signal: three dots and three dashes and three dots again. At first, Eldon thought he was seeing things, but the tiny light kept flashing the same signal over and over again. Out of habit, Eldon looked down and noted the date and time on his watch. He reached up and pushed the overhead button to summon a stewardess.

Presently, a stewardess whose name tag read "Kathie" appeared. "Can I help you?" she said with a smile.

Sheriff Fogus replied, "Ma'am, I just saw an SOS signal out my window just before I called. It seemed to be some sort of signal light. I think that it needs to be reported." Kathie made a short nervous laugh and stated, "At this altitude that would be impossible. You must have just seen a reflection."

What happened next took Kathie aback. The countenance of the passenger in front of her changed immediately. He looked at her with a dead serious face and stated, "Lady, I want to see the captain of this airplane. I am not making a joke. I want some assurance that what I am reporting is going to be reported. You are wasting my time now. Do as I requested!"

The tone of the passenger's voice and his demeanor scared Kathie. She decided to report the incident to the pilot. Shortly, the first officer whose name tag read "Greg" appeared. Greg was a boy wonder graduate of flight school. He was top in his class. Most recently, he had attended a training course on how to handle disputes with passengers and as usual graduated with a high score. He was eager to try out his newly learned skills.

Greg approached Eldon and stated, "Hi, I am the first officer Greg Hamlin. I understand that you have a concern that you want to express to us. How can I be of assistance?"

Eldon repeated his observations to Greg. Greg gave a small smile and stated, "Sir, I'm sure that you believe what you saw and, of course, if there was such a signal and I was in your place, I would want it reported as well. I certainly commend you for providing us with the information. I must assure you that at this altitude, it would not be possible to see such a signal. We will, however, take the information and pass it along to our operations center when we land."

Greg suddenly found himself nose to nose with a rather large muscular person. His eyes were a steely blue gray. His voice was like iron and authoritative. He spoke in a very quiet, calm, and almost inaudible voice which penetrated to Greg's very soul like a small still voice.

"Listen, you pencil-pushing little asshole, I know what I saw. I am law enforcement, and here is my badge and ID. If you do not report what I saw immediately, I am going to have your ass. If there is someone down there who needs help and you are refusing to alert the proper authorities, I will see that the family of that person sues you personally and this airline. I will personally go to hell and back to testify against you on behalf of the family. Above all, I will see that the media is notified, and I will stand and shout before the cameras how you refused to help. Now why don't you go back to the pilot's cabin and call this in before I really lose my temper!"

At that point, Greg decided that perhaps he should not piss off this individual. This man's whole countenance indicated that he was quite capable of enforcing his demands. Besides, the class had taught him to defuse the situation and give the customer what he wanted if it was possible. Greg decided to take down the information and the passenger's name and forward it on. It was better to report the incident than to argue. If the passenger was right, and he failed to report it, he would be in trouble. If there was nothing to the report, then the passenger would look like a fool. Greg took the information, thanked Eldon, and went back to the cabin to make his report to the captain.

Captain Lysen was a twenty-year veteran flying jumbo jets. In addition to flying planes, he was the past president of the pilots association. When he spoke, people listened. As far as physical appearances went, he was not tall dark and handsome as the media portrayed pilots. He was average height with a stout frame. His eyes were steel blue with heavy black eyebrows. When he spoke, he spoke as one with authority and experience.

Captain Lysen had two problems. First, he had to contend with turbulence and the second was he had to deal with Greg who was the son of the chairman of the board of the airline. Captain Lysen viewed Greg as a Mama's boy who had everything handed to him. Secretly, he wanted to throw the little twit out the window at ten thousand feet.

When Greg told Captain Lysen about the passenger's story and the fact that he was law enforcement, the captain initially did not respond. Captain Lysen's first thought was, "Wonder boy could not even pacify a disgruntled passenger who could not possibly have seen a signal this far up in the sky." Then the captain remembered that he had seen and spoken to the passenger. The person did not seem to be a nut case. In fact, the passenger seemed to be a decent person. Captain Lysen decided to make a formal report instead of taking a skeptical attitude. Besides, he did not want to be responsible if the passenger was right. He instructed the navigator to transmit the coordinates and a report of the incident to their base in Honolulu.

Just as a public relations shot, Captain Lysen asked Kathie to go and tell the passenger that the report had been radioed in. When Eldon got the news, he thanked the stewardess and turned to stare out the window.

CHAPTER 4

Coast Guard Honolulu

Petty Officer First Class Wayne Ferguson's tour of duty had just started. He had his usual cup of coffee and a bagel ready to devour. Just as he was getting ready to take his first bite into the bagel, his phone rang. Ferguson rolled his eyes and put down the bagel and reached for the phone.

Ferguson answered, "United States Coast Guard Petty Officer Ferguson speaking."

A rather pleasant female voice was on the line from an airline. The woman asked for the duty officer.

Petty Officer Ferguson replied, "The duty officer is not here at the moment, ma'am. I am in charge."

The voice on the phone identified herself as Rachael Moss of Pacific Airlines. She stated, "A passenger on one of our flights headed to Honolulu has reported seeing an SOS signal. We are not sure what to make of it. The passenger was quite adamant about what he saw. As a precaution, we decided to take the information and forward it to the Coast Guard in the event that there was some merit to the passenger's claim. I might add that the passenger seems to be rational and is law enforcement from the State of Idaho."

"She can't be serious," thought Petty Officer Ferguson.

Protocol did mandate that all such information be taken even if it was somewhat dubious. Petty Officer Ferguson took the information and thanked the caller.

He hung up, then sat back to think about what he had just been told. The story itself was implausible. It is near impossible to see a manual distress signal using a mirror from three miles up in the air.

Yet the airline captain had decided that there was some merit to the sighting; otherwise, he would not have made the report. Stranger things have happened.

Petty Officer Ferguson prepared an incident report to take to his watch commander. The watch commander was Cdr. Lawrence Rogers, a fifteen-year veteran of the United States Coast Guard. His duties included screening all calls for assistance and determining what course of action to recommend. He was getting ready to call his wife when Petty Officer Ferguson knocked on his door.

Somewhat irritated at the interruption, Commander Rogers stated abruptly, "Come in."

Petty Officer Ferguson entered, saluted, and stated, "Sir, we have a report of a boat in distress or at most some people needing help in a lifeboat. The report comes through Pacific Airlines and was phoned into us by their communication office."

Commander Rogers listened to the report with some amusement. Finally, he said, "Let me get this straight. A passenger on an airliner twenty thousand feet in the air reports to the airline captain that he has seen an SOS signal from possibly a signal mirror or some such device and expects us to initiate a search for the possibility that someone is in need of assistance. They can't be serious!"

Petty Officer Ferguson and the commander had a good working relationship. There were times that the commander had listened to the petty officer's advice and had found that the advice was sound. This time, Petty Officer Ferguson paused then stated, "May I speak, sir?"

Commander Rogers stated, "Go ahead."

"Sir, it seems to me that the airline is simply covering their rears. If the information turns out to be true, then the airline is off the hook. If the information is not good, then the airline has done its duty in reporting the incident. If we ignore the information and it turns out to be true, then we are the bad guys, not the airline. If the information is not true, then we need not worry. However, I might point out that this route is quite often taken by small sailing craft that sail out of Ensenada, Mexico, to the Hawaiian Islands. Perhaps we should send out a request for information to points along the West Coast of the United States and Mexico. If we do not get any responses to our request, then we can claim that we did take action and did not find anything. If we do get a response, then we can take the appropriate action. An inquiry will not cost anything and will take little time."

Commander Rogers thought for a second, then replied, "You are right. Given today's climate for finding and blaming anyone to cover your rear, maybe we should at least make the minimum effort. You make up a simple request for information and send it out to all stations under my signature. Let me know if you get any results."

Petty Officer Ferguson stated, "Yes, Sir." He then turned and left.

Commander Rogers returned to his phone call. He had to make dinner arrangements with his wife and her parents. He did not need an almost ridiculous distraction such as what he had just been told.

Jan, his wife, was on top of things as usual. She had the restaurant picked out and reservations made. Satisfied that all was going well, Commander Rogers settled in to take care of the usual pile of paperwork. He would hurry to get all of it done so he could leave early to meet his wife's parents at the airport and take them home.

Petty Officer Ferguson typed up a short request for information and sent it to the communications center through a computer link for transmission. It read:

"TO: Communique priority 2D82 all stations on West Coast of the United States and Mexico. Reply code 3Z8T.

FROM: United States Coast Guard Station, Honolulu, Hawaii, USA

We have a report of a boat possibly in distress in the area of Grid 3BK19.

Please advise if you have any report of an overdue boat or any report of a boat requesting assistance or if you are attempting the rescue of any boat in that area at this time. Please reply to: Cdr. Lawrence Rogers, United States Coast Guard, Honolulu, USA. Thank you in advance for your cooperation.

End of message."

Throughout the worldwide maritime emergency services, requests for information on overdue boats are routine. The vast majority of the reports turn out to be some relative who is concerned for a loved one who has not contacted them. Usually, the boater has just failed to call home. Sometimes, information is developed through these routine inquiries that raise an alarm and further action is needed. Such was the case of the *Nadia Marie*.

Generally, routine inquiries are placed in an in basket or left on a desk for some low-level subordinate to act on. Sometimes any reply to an inquiry will take a couple of days to a week before the request is acted on depending on the information received. In this case, the reply was almost immediate. Within a couple of hours, Petty Officer Ferguson received a reply for Commander Rogers from the Coast Guard based in Seattle Washington. It read:

"TO: Commander L. Rogers United States Coast Guard, Honolulu

FROM: United States Coast Guard Headquarters, Seattle, Washington

IN RE: Request for information your number 3Z8T

We have received a report of an overdue boat named the Nadia Marie. Our complainant is a nanny of the boat owners; a John and Julie Schwartz of Seattle, Washington. The boat was due your location approximately ten days ago. We did send a request for information to the Honolulu Customs station. Customs has advised that the boat has not reported in as required. Our information is that the Nadia Marie was to leave Ensenada, Mexico, about a month ago and travel to Honolulu. The Schwartz family has not been heard from since. We received the report last night and have not had the time to send out a general inquiry. Let us know if you wish for us to handle the matter or if you wish to take the initiative.

End of message."

Petty Officer Ferguson sent an e-mail to Commander Rogers. It read: "Sir, we have received a message from headquarters in Seattle that they have a report of a missing boat named the *Nadia Marie* that may have left Ensenada, Mexico, within a month and has not been heard from since. The *Nadia Marie* was en route to our location. Seattle advises that our Honolulu Customs has no record of the *Nadia Marie* registering here in Honolulu. Would you like me to send an amended message to Ensenada and West Coast locations asking for information on the *Nadia Marie*?"

The reply e-mail was short and brief. It read: "Please send the amended request and keep me advised. Commander Rogers."

Petty Officer Ferguson had a revised request transmitted. It read:

"TO: West Coast locations and to La Oficina de Administracion la Aduana en Ensenada, Mexico

FROM: United States Coast Guard, Honolulu

IN RE: Request for information our reference number 3Z8T

This is an updated request for information concerning our earlier request for information. We are requesting information on a boat the Nadia Marie registered to a John and Julie Schwartz of Seattle, Washington, USA. We believe this boat may have been last seen in Ensenada, Mexico. Any station, particularly the Ensenada Customs that may have information on this boat is asked to contact this station. Please send all information attention to the Commander L. Rogers, United States Coast Guard, Honolulu.

End of Message."

When such a message is received, it triggers an unwritten alert that something may be wrong and that there may be a vessel in trouble. All stations immediately begin to check their records to determine if there is any information on the boat in question.

It did not take long for Petty Officer Ferguson to track the movements of the *Nadia Marie*. He was able through information received to piece together the route of the *Nadia Marie*. He ascertained that the *Nadia Marie* had left Miami en route to the Panama Canal. A Coast Guard cutter reported it had stopped the *Nadia Marie* for a drug check near Mexican waters off the coast of Texas. Then stations along the Atlantic and Pacific replied with information on the *Nadia Marie* and its travels. At the Panama Canal, the *Nadia Marie* and several boats were logged as having gone through the canal.

Various resort locations along the coast of Mexico reported the *Nadia Marie* staying in port. Confirmation that the *Nadia Marie* had been in Ensenada came in a message that read:

"TO: United States Coast Guard, Honolulu, USA

Attn: Commander L. Rogers

FROM: El Servicio de Administracion Triburaria, Hacienda, La Oficina Aduana de Ciudad Ensenada de los Estados Unidos de Mexico

INRE: Request for information your number 3Z8T

Our records indicate that a forty-five foot boat named the Nadia Marie which is owned by a John and Julie Schwartz registered with our office located at the Hotel Coral and Marina on June 16. The boat and owners left the Hotel Coral en route to Honolulu, Hawaii, USA, on June 20. End of Message."

CHAPTER 5

"El Poster de los Angeles de la Estacion Militar de los Estados Unidos de Mexico."

Every nation that has a border on the oceans of the world has communication stations to monitor maritime traffic. "El Poster de los Angeles de la Estacion Militar" was located in Baja California. Its job was to monitor maritime traffic and coordinate rescue efforts if needed on the West Coast of Mexico. Sometimes it assisted the Mexican and United States drug enforcement agencies as well.

The first message received from the Honolulu Coast Guard did not get much attention. The second message received a much higher priority due to its specific information.

Capitan Miguel Angel Antonio Lopez Canal Flores commanded the communications center. He remembered an incident about a month earlier where a garbled transmission was received from an unknown source requesting assistance. Capitan Flores had an aide pull the record for review. A message was sent to the US Coast Guard, Honolulu.

Petty Officer Ferguson received the message from Capitan Flores. It read:

"*TO: United States Guard Honolulu*

Attn: Commander L. Rogers

FROM: El Poster de los Angeles de la Estacion Militar de los Estados Unidos de Mexico, Capitan Miguel Angel Antonio Lopez Canal Flores Comandante

IN RE: Request for information your reference number 3Z8T

We have some information that may pertain to your request for information on a boat named the Nadia Marie. On June 26, this station received a garbled transmission from a vessel that claimed to be in distress. The message was fragmented, and we were not able to make contact with the vessel. We have pulled the records of the incident along with a tape of the garbled transmission. The transmission sounded like the vessel in distress had Marie, Maru, or Maria in its name. An alert was sent out to local stations asking if anyone else had received the message. No other station had received the transmission. There was no report of any overdue boats received, so the information was noted and filed. We do have the audio of the transmission. If you will provide us with an e-mail, we will transmit the information to you. Please advise if this information is needed or helpful. End of Message."

Petty Officer Ferguson immediately sent a message back to Captain Flores asking that he send the audio of the radio transmission. When Petty Officer Ferguson got the audio tape of the SOS transmission, he had the communications center filter it to try to make it more understandable. When he got the results from the communications center, Petty Officer Ferguson put together a report to submit to Commander Rogers as soon as possible.

CHAPTER 6

The Decision

Petty Officer Ferguson knocked on Commander Rogers's door and was admitted promptly. He approached the commander's desk and stated, "Sir, we have received two messages from authorities in Mexico and one from Seattle on that missing boat that you might want to read immediately."

The petty officer then handed the messages to the commander and waited for a reply.

Commander Rogers read the messages then reread them again. Finally, he looked up at the Petty Officer. "All this information is a little thin to order a full-scale search for this boat or its occupants, especially when all we have to go on is the possible sighting of an SOS signal seen by an airline passenger twenty thousand feet in the air. We are not sure we even have a starting point or even a missing boat in distress." The commander then paused for a response from Petty Officer Ferguson.

"Sir, as I see it, we have several problems with this incident," replied Petty Officer Ferguson. "First you have the problem with the total information. I had the Mexican commander of the communications center that recorded the SOS e-mail us a copy of the radio transmission they received. Our communications center filtered it the best they could. It definitely was a female voice speaking English. What audio we did get clearly indicated that the boat was sinking and she was requesting assistance. The entire name of the boat was inaudible, but the word *Marie* was clear. It is my opinion based on all the reports that the owner of the *Nadia Marie* was the one who transmitted the SOS and that the boat was sinking.

"Then you have the confirmation from Mexican Customs in Ensenada, Mexico, confirming that the *Nadia Marie* did register and leave the port a few days later. Finally, you have the report out of Seattle that the *Nadia Marie* is overdue."

"Customs here in Honolulu does not show any record of the *Nadia Marie* reporting in upon arrival. She should have arrived days ago."

"Next, you have a problem with the distance. If the sighting by the airline passenger is correct, then you are at the point of no return for aircraft. Even our Orions could not get there and perform a search."

"Then you have a weather problem. The weather service advises that there is a typhoon headed into that area. By late tomorrow afternoon, the storm will pass through the area. No one in a life raft can survive in that kind of storm."

"There is one option. There is a naval task force on maneuvers in the area that could reach the area and maybe rescue survivors if they can be located. The task force does have reconnaissance planes that could perform the search. If one of the ships that carry rescue helicopters could get within reach of the survivors, then they could rescue the people in the life raft. It would be very close."

Commander Rogers looked at Petty Officer Ferguson and thought that if this guy ever wanted to attend the naval academy, he would be the first to recommend him. He could see why this individual had reached the rank of petty officer first class in a little less than one hitch. Commander Rogers thought he would make every effort to keep this person in the Coast Guard.

After a brief pause, Commander Rogers stated to Petty Officer Ferguson, "Since this is going to require coordination between the navy and ourselves, we will have to involve the admiral in the overall decision. Do we know where he is?"

Petty Officer Ferguson replied, "I believe he is at the Kahani Dinner Club having a late breakfast with several people including the Commander in Chief Pacific of the navy Adm. Steve Bender, sir."

"Good! I will take it from here. Would you send in Lieutenant Storm."

Petty Officer Ferguson replied, "Aye, sir," then saluted, made an about face, and left the commander's office.

CHAPTER 7

The Breakfast

Once-a-week breakfast was a tradition for the Commander in Chief Pacific, or CINCPAC, Adm. Steve Bender and United States Coast Guard Vice Admiral Wayne Hutcherson.

Their breakfast had been intruded upon by having to host a working session to discuss search and rescue and natural disaster policies. Both admirals had their aides with them. Representing the governor's office was the governor's chief of staff. There were representatives from the state legislature, the army, and the Federal Emergency Management Agency or FEMA.

None of the participants knew that the FEMA representative was also a CIA agent named Andrew "Andy" Wilson who had been sent to Hawaii on a special assignment.

A discussion on tsunami evacuation plans was in progress when Lieutenant Storm of the US Coast came into the room and approached the aide to Vice Admiral Hutcherson. The aide, a Lieutenant Keyes, got up and went to the other side of the room with Lieutenant Storm in order to not interrupt the meeting.

The two men conferred for a brief moment, then Lieutenant Keyes returned to the table and whispered to the admiral, "Sir, the Coast Guard operations duty officer is here and has a matter of some importance that needs your attention."

Admiral Hutcherson stood and said, "Will you excuse me a moment, ladies and gentlemen. I have a small matter to attend to."

He then went over to where Lieutenant Storm was standing. Lieutenant Storm related the story of the *Nadia Maria* from the original sighting by an airline passenger to the Mexican reports and the report filed in Seattle. Lieutenant Storm also told the admiral about the typhoon warning for the area.

Admiral Hutcherson then returned to the table where the group had paused to see if the admiral was going to share his secret with them.

Admiral Hutcherson thought for a moment, then turned to Admiral Bender and said, "Admiral, I have just received a request from our operations center to ask the navy for assistance in a rescue attempt."

Admiral Bender looked at his friend and stated, "What is the circumstance?"

"It is something of an unbelievable story. It appears that an airline passenger spotted an SOS signal from twenty thousand feet in the air. That information was relayed to us by the airline. We sent out a routine inquiry just in case. We got a message from a Mexican communications center located in Baja California advising they had picked up a garbled transmission of a boat in distress about a month ago. They were unable to track the call. A local inquiry did not turn up anything, so the Mexicans filed the incident away. Our Seattle headquarters received a report of an overdue boat headed here from Ensenada, Mexico, two days ago. Ensenada Customs confirms that the boat, the *Nadia Marie*, registered there then left four days later headed for Honolulu. We checked with the local customs here who advised that the boat has not registered here. We also had the Mexican commander of the Baja communications center send us a copy of the tape of the distress call they received. According to our communications center, the tape did show that a boat was in distress and that a partial name of the boat was 'Marie.' The person on the tape sounded like a female speaking English."

Admiral Hutcherson continued, "Our operations center is of the opinion that there was a boat in distress. All we have for a location is the sighting of the SOS signal by an airline passenger twenty thousand feet in the air. This whole operation would depend on that sighting. The location is at the point of no return for any aircraft. However, the navy does have a task force on maneuvers in the area that could perform a search if you authorized it."

Admiral Bender frowned, then looked at his old friend and stated, "That is not much information to go on. Given that there is a boat in distress, we do not have a good location. A sighting by an airline passenger twenty thousand feet in the air is really questionable. We would be asked to undertake an expensive search with no assurance that the location is accurate."

Then, as an afterthought, the admiral turned to the people at the table and said, "Okay, ladies and gentlemen, you have heard the story and underlying facts, what would you do in this situation?"

Immediately a general discussion broke out among those at the table. Most at the table did not pay attention when Andy Wilson excused himself from the table as if he was going to the men's room. On his way out of the room, he passed by Lieutenant Storm.

He called the Lieutenant by name and asked, "Can you tell me what quadrant the airline passenger sighting was in?"

Lieutenant Storm replied, "It was in quadrant 3BK19, sir." "Thank you, Lieutenant," replied Andy.

CHAPTER 8

The Photo

Andy Wilson was in Honolulu to monitor and assess a new secret satellite system that very few people knew existed. It was code named "Martha." This new system could penetrate to a depth of five hundred feet below the ocean surface. On ground, it could penetrate to a depth of hundred feet. Martha was designed to counter a new sub built by the Chinese. These subs were a stealth-type sub that were virtually undetectable. Martha could find and track and help neutralize the threat.

The *Nadia Marie* incident could prove the value of the system since the "Martha" system was unproven. Andy had been sent to monitor any foreign submarines that would try and monitor the task force just to see how accurate "Martha" was.

Andy walked to a point to where he could not be seen by the others and to a secluded part of the club. He pulled out an encrypted and secure cell phone and dialed a number.

The person on the other end of the phone answered, "Blumenthals, how may I help you?"

Andy replied, "This is representative 3584SPD, may I have extension 101, please."

"Thank you, sir, one moment, please," came the reply. There were two rings, then a voice said, "Stanford."

"Dick, this is Andy in Honolulu. I have come across a perfect test for Martha. It seems there is a missing boat owned by a family from Seattle. There has been a sighting of an SOS signal that might belong to the boat, but the sighting is unconfirmed. Why don't we have Zoe run a quick scan and see if we can determine if the boat is in the area?"

Dick replied, "Sure, let's give it a try and see what happens. Stand by a second while I get Zoe on the line."

There was a short wait, then a click. Dick came on and stated, "Zoe, are you there?"

Zoe replied, "I'm here."

"Andy, are you there?'

"I'm here."

"Okay, Andy, tell Zoe what you have and let's see what happens."

Andy began, "Zoe, we are looking for a small forty-foot boat or a life raft in naval quadrant 3BK19 or maybe in the surrounding quadrants. Can you pull that area up and see if you can locate the boat or life raft?"

"Stand by, Andy," said Zoe. "It will only take a couple of seconds." Andy and Dick could hear the keyboard clicking as Zoe typed.

Within seconds, she came back on the line.

"Okay, guys, you are not going to believe this. Here it comes."

Zoe sent the video picture to Andy and Dick. Andy looked at the photo and drew a sharp breath. Finally, he said to Dick, "We need to do something to help."

Dick replied, "What do you suggest?"

Andy began, "There is a problem with the authorization to send out the navy to search. Admiral Bender is skeptical and has started a roundtable discussion among the emergency management group that I am eating breakfast with over what action to take. I am afraid he will not approve the request. He is treating this as an academic question. We need to take some action to encourage him to authorize the search. Here is what I think.

"Why don't we have our resident computer guru and hacker send this picture to the Pentagon communications center. We can route it through the White House Situation Room to the Pentagon. A note briefly stating 'please take action on this,' can be attached to the message.

"Once the Pentagon communications center gets the picture and the note, they will have to act on the information, especially if we put a Joint Chiefs authorization on the message."

All agreed to the plan. However, Richard Stanford had another idea as well.

CHAPTER 9

The Situation Room Message

When Andy sat back down at the table, still there was a lively discussion going on over a rescue search for the boat. Lieutenant Storm was still standing a respectful distance in the background watching. Lieutenant Keyes had returned to his seat near Admiral Hutcherson.

Within a couple of minutes, a cell phone belonging to the aide for Admiral Bender, a lieutenant named Davis, began to buzz. The lieutenant quietly pulled his phone out to see a text message displayed. It read:

> *"We have a priority message for Admiral Bender from the Joint Chiefs at the White House Situation Room, can you have the admiral contact us ASAP… CINCPAC Operations Center."*

Lieutenant Davis got up from his chair and quietly went over to where Admiral Bender was sitting with a bemused look on his face as he listened to the debate. Lieutenant Davis bent over and whispered to the admiral.

> *"Sir, you have a priority message from the Joint Chiefs originating from the White House Situation Room. Our ops center is asking you to contact them immediately." Admiral Bender stood and said to the group, "Gentlemen, excuse me for a moment. I have to make a call."*
>
> *Admiral Bender went to the hallway with his aide following. He pushed a button on his cell phone which connected him to his operations center. A voice came on the line and stated, "Operations center, Lieutenant Canby."*

> "Lieutenant Canby, this is Admiral Bender. I have a message to call the center for a priority message."
>
> "Yes, sir," replied the lieutenant. "Would you like us to text the message to you or do you want to have us read the body of the message to you? There is a picture that accompanies the message that will have to be viewed in person or by you on your cell phone. It is up to you."
>
> Admiral Bender replied, "Text the message to me and send the picture to my cell phone as well."

Within a couple of seconds, the admiral's text message icon started flashing on his cell phone. He told the lieutenant that the message was coming through, and he would call him back. The admiral pushed his text message button to see the message. It read:

> "From the headquarters of the Joint Chief of Staff's White House Situation Room Station 8 and the Pentagon communications division, authorization WHSR82ZN91. You are directed to initiate a search and rescue attempt in Quadrant 3BK19 sector D to rescue three souls believed to be the survivors of a boating accident. You are to take personal charge of the rescue attempt and see it through to its conclusion. Attached to this message is a photo for your information. It was taken by satellite within the last two hours. At the completion of your mission, you are to report your findings and actions to this office. In addition, you are directed to periodically update this office on your progress. Direct all messages to WHSR830Martha.
>
> End of Message."

Admiral Bender pushed the attachment button on his message. A picture of a small girl in a life raft appeared on his screen. The little girl appeared disheveled and was looking skyward with tears streaming down her cheeks. There appeared to be a woman and another person in the background partially covered by a tarp.

Admiral Bender again dialed the operations center and spoke to Lieutenant Canby.

"Lieutenant, have you verified the authorization code in this message?"

Lieutenant Canby replied, "Yes, sir, we have. The authorization code is properly verified. I am not sure who Martha is, however, but it does originate from the White House Situation Room under the authority of the Joint Chiefs of Staff. Also, the code does indicate that the president of the United States is involved. If you examine the authorization code closely, you see that it ends in a one. That number means that the office of the president of the United States is involved either by issuing the order or has approved the order."

Admiral Bender thanked the lieutenant and hung up. Admiral Bender returned to his seat and sat down. The group had become silent and was waiting for the admiral to speak. Finally, Admiral Bender looked at the group and stated, "Gentlemen, I think we have pretty much covered all the items on our agenda. My second in command will follow up on what we have discussed today. If you run into any problems, contact my office, and we will try and resolve the problem immediately. Again, thank you for coming."

"I need to speak to Admiral Hutcherson. Admiral, would you stay for a moment?" The admiral stood and shook hands with each person as they exited the room.

After the group had left, Admiral Bender turned to Admiral Hutcherson and said, "Take a look at the message and picture I received a few minutes ago." Admiral Bender handed his cell phone to Admiral Hutcherson.

Admiral Hutcherson read the message and looked at the satellite photo. He slowly handed the phone back to Admiral Bender. There was a pause, then Admiral Hutcherson stated, "Good lord, that little girl is as old as my granddaughter Olivia. What she must be feeling at this moment is indescribable."

Admiral Bender turned to Lieutenant Davis and ordered, "Lieutenant, you are to prepare a message to Admiral Strange of Task Force Tango. He is ordered to attempt to rescue this little girl and her family. He is to take personal charge of the operation and report directly to me. Also advise Admiral Strange that he is to update me periodically. Prepare the order under my authority immediately."

Lieutenant Davis came to his feet and stated, "Aye, sir," and left the room.

CHAPTER 10

Life on the Raft

John Schwartz had been hurt more than he let on. When he finally came to his full senses, he found himself in the life raft under a tarp. His head was throbbing, and his vision was blurred. He became aware of his wife's voice that was reassuring their daughter that everything would be all right and that Daddy was okay.

He tried to sit up, but when he did, he became dizzy. He lay back and called to his wife and daughter. Both turned to him and gave him a hug. It didn't take long for John to assess the predicament they were in. They were in the middle of nowhere without immediate assistance. The wind had subsided, and the rain was down to a fine mist.

The immediate concern was water and food. An inventory of the supplies showed a little over a week's supply of food and water. Both would have to be rationed to stretch out as long as possible in case rescue would not be coming soon.

John cut his ration of food and water to give more to his wife and daughter. Ultimately, this decision would cause him to become a liability to the family effort to survive. He had no way of knowing that the blow to his head not only gave him a concussion but had caused a small brain hemorrhage. The injury and brain damage would eventually cause him to lose consciousness.

Julie knew she had to be strong to live. When she realized the boat was sinking, she took stock of the situation and began to organize. She had Nadia collect the first aid supplies to treat her husband. Then she set about collecting life jackets and a tarp to protect them from the storm.

Once the supplies were collected, she inflated the life raft and stowed the supplies inside. She was able to get her husband and Nadia into the life raft. All of this was done while the boat was rocking and listing badly. Just as they pulled away from the boat, the boat rolled over onto its side.

As the days passed, Julie cut her own rations to give more to Nadia. John had passed out and was of no help. Julie had to force John to take water and some food. She began to feel the effects of limiting her water and food in order to give more to Nadia. Sometimes she would sleep for long periods of time. Dehydration began to take its toll.

One day, Julie was given aid by Mother Nature. A small squall developed which gave Julie a chance to collect water using the tarp. The water helped, but the food was getting low, and it was a matter of a couple of days before it would be gone.

Depression began to creep into Julie's mind. She began to think that it would have been more merciful if all of them had drowned than face a slow death under the sun on an open ocean.

Nadia had been a godsend to her mother. She helped with the boat as they sailed across the open ocean. When the boat began to sink, Nadia helped her mother collect supplies and put them into the life raft. She even helped put her father into the raft.

As the days passed, Nadia found ways to pass away the time. She invented toys out of the ration packages. She even had a small doll she had managed to salvage. Nadia had found a signal mirror in the emergency kit. The signal itself was an enhanced system of magnifying glasses and mirrors to boost its signal. When airplanes passed overhead, she would signal the plane using the signal mirror. She had learned the international code for SOS from girl scouts.

When her mother began to deteriorate, Nadia made sure that her mother would drink her ration of water daily and eat some food. She would force her father to drink and eat when he had a period where he was somewhat conscious.

One day, she told her mother that she had a dream that lots of big ships were coming to find them and take them home. Her mother hugged her tight and began to cry. When Nadia told Julie about the dream, her mother felt in her heart that Nadia was beginning to become dehydrated and starting to hallucinate. Julie prayed that death would take them quickly.

CHAPTER 11

Task Force Tango

Adm. Jack Strange was a throwback to the fighting men of old. Some had suggested that he belonged in the Victorian Age. He was a strict disciplinarian and did not tolerate immoral conduct in his personal and professional life. If a sailor under his command was caught breaking the rules, there was a swift and immediate punishment waiting for the miscreant.

The admiral had come up through the ranks. He was a petty officer first class by the time he was twenty. His proficiency ratings were so high that he was given the opportunity to go to the naval academy which he accepted with immense gratitude. He graduated from the academy among the top five cadets.

Ensign Strange developed an early reputation for strictness and proficiency. Early on, he showed his ability to adapt tactics to the situation. This earned him the admiration of his superiors.

Once he commanded his own ship, Strange delighted in forcing Russian or Chinese submarines to surface after failing to shake the pursing Strange. Once he almost created an incident. He detected a submarine shadowing his ship. Strange promptly took after the unidentified submarine. After a few hours, the submarine was forced to surface. Strange was getting ready to circle the vessel, as was his custom, when the submarine captain scrambled his gun crew and fired a shot in the vicinity of Strange's destroyer. Strange immediately backed off to give the submarine captain some room so as not to provoke him further. It turned out the sub was a North Korean sub whose commander had a short fuse and even less tolerance of the cat and mouse game Strange had been playing with his sub and crew.

Besides, the sub captain had to save some face. Strange let him have his moment of glory and pulled back to his regular patrol area. He knew who had won, and the captain of the North Korean sub knew who had won the contest.

Following the North Korean sub incident, Strange was ordered to tone down his zeal for going after the opposition before he inadvertently started a war. His actions soon came to the attention of the Russian and Chinese intelligence services. Wherever Strange was assigned, an intelligence officer from China or Russia was not too far away. The intelligence surveillance on Strange was so intense at times that a Russian intelligence officer drove the limousine that took Strange and his wife to the airport to go on vacation one year.

Admiral Strange had a reputation as a brilliant tactician and a superb administrator. He was equally at home sitting in a computer chair as he was at sitting in a captain's chair on a warship. Adm. Jack Strange was in charge of a navy task force code named Tango. Under his present command, he had two aircraft carriers and their accompanying vessels. He had been tasked to divide the two aircraft carrier groups in two and conduct war simulation games.

Accompanying this task force was an international force consisting of ships from Australia, New Zealand, and Japan. One of the purposes of the task force was to learn to coordinate efforts between nations in the Southeast Asia region.

There was a hidden agenda which Admiral Strange was not aware of. Admiral Strange was in his private quarters when the message came. There was a knock on his door.

He stated, "Come in."

A young ensign entered the quarters and addressed the admiral. "Sir, you have a priority message from CINCPAC," stated the ensign. He then handed the message to the admiral. The message read:

> *"Headquarters Commander in Chief Pacific priority alpha three sierra CINCPAC one hotel six to Adm. Jack Strange, commander of Task Force Tango. Authorization 6CX82YW. You are directed to launch an immediate search and rescue attempt in quadrant 3BK19 with emphasis on sector Delta of that quadrant. You are to effect the rescue of three persons believed to be in a life raft and render all aid and assistance to them. It is imperative that you*

act quickly. There is a typhoon moving into the area by 1600 hours Honolulu time tomorrow afternoon.

You are directed to periodically report your progress to this headquarters. Further you are to take direct control of this mission and supervise its operations to its conclusion. Adm. Steven Bender, Commander in Chief Pacific.
End of Message"

Admiral Strange did not believe that a whole task force was being diverted from training to perform a rescue operation. He looked at the ensign and asked, "Has this message been authenticated?"

The ensign replied, "Aye, sir. If you look closely at the authorization code, you will notice that the order originated from a higher headquarters than CINCPAC."

Admiral Strange's eyebrows raised slightly, then he looked at the ensign and ordered, "On your way out, will you have my aide ask Captain Kimmel to report to me as soon as possible?"

The ensign came to attention, saluted, and said, "Aye, sir." He then turned and left the admiral's quarters. A few minutes later, Captain Kimmel knocked on the door. Admiral Strange had him come in. He had Captain Kimmel read the orders he had received from CINCPAC. After reading the orders, Captain Kimmel looked up at the admiral.

Captain Kimmel asked, "Am I to assume that CINCPAC wants us to drop our training mission and go do a search and rescue?"

"That is my interpretation of the orders," said Admiral Strange.

"Well, it would be a good indication on how well we could perform," said Captain Kimmel. "It certainly would be a test to see how quickly we can divert this force on a moment's notice to seek out and find another objective."

"What do we have in the way of men and material that we can send out to begin the search?" asked Admiral Strange.

"Right now, sir, we have a reconnaissance crew here in quarters. The other crews are out looking for Bravo Group. As you know, our objective was to locate and destroy Bravo Group. Admiral Harney is living up to his grandfather's reputation. He went to the starting coordinates as ordered in the mission training plan. However, the training plan did not say that he could not show up early. The admiral showed up early and has vanished with his entire command. We are now on the defensive looking for him. We should find his group soon.

Admiral Strange's eyes narrowed to slits, and his face turned red. He was not about to be outwitted by his second in command. He would get even. In spite of this latest revelation, Admiral Strange kept focused on the orders at hand. He paused for a moment, then stated, "We can launch the search using the recon plane we have on hand, but we still need to get a rescue ship close enough to launch aircraft that can actually perform the rescue."

Captain Kimmel said, "Sir, we could detach our fastest ship and have it go ahead at flank speed. Traveling all night and into tomorrow afternoon should get them within range so that the rescue helicopters could make the rescue. We are restricted by the speed of our support ships and will not make it in time."

"That is a good plan, Captain. We will get our carrier group turned around and proceed. While we are at it, I intend to teach my second in command a lesson in tactics. He will never find us before we find him. I will sneak up and kick him in the butt before he knows what hit him. Let's recall our other recon planes as soon as possible so that they may be used in the search as well."

Captain Kimmel came to attention, saluted, and said, "Aye, sir," then left.

Admiral Strange did not know that his second in command had already found him. The rules of engagement specified that no military satellites would be used in this exercise. The second in command, Admiral Harney, simply had his communications people tap into a civilian system and was using it to locate Admiral Strange. All he did was go to Google Earth. The mission referees had to agree that no mission rule was being violated.

CHAPTER 12

The Rescue Vessels

Captain Kimmel issued orders immediately to have his recon planes recalled. An order was given to have the one reconnaissance flight crew on board report to the flight briefing room immediately.

Admiral Strange's chief of staff notified the captains of the *USS Alabama* and the *USS Cobb* to stand by for a conference call in twenty minutes. The *USS Alabama* was a light cruiser, and the *USS Cobb* was its support ship, a destroyer escort. Both vessels were the fastest ships in the fleet.

Cdr. Jim Harris and Lt. Cdr. Tom Riley were just taking it easy after a long recon mission to try and locate Bravo Group of Task Force Tango. Bravo Group was the enemy and had to be found before they found Alpha Group. Both pilots shared the same quarters. They had developed a personal and team relationship that formed an excellent working relationship. Their crew was the best in the fleet.

Commander Harris was writing his daily e-mails to his wife and children. He could not send the e-mails for a while since the admiral had imposed a total blackout to prevent Bravo Group from discovering them through their electronic transmissions.

Lieutenant Commander Riley had just returned from lifting weights and was getting ready to take a shower. A message came across the intercom directing the two and their crew to report to the flight briefing room. Waiting for the group was Commander Spencer assigned to flight operations. Commander Spencer greeted the group and had them take their seats. He then conducted a briefing on the mission that was being assigned to them.

"Good afternoon, gentlemen. We have been directed by CINCPAC to try and rescue a family in a life raft in quadrant 3BK19. I am sure you are aware of the distance involved here. Our only hope of finding this family is to use you to try and locate the raft. Once the raft is located, we will then try to close the distance so that rescue vessels and aircraft can make the rescue. Keep in mind that time is not on our side. There is a typhoon approaching that quadrant and will pass through by approximately 1600 hours tomorrow afternoon. You will barely have enough time to reach the area and film the entire quadrant before dark. We have ordered our other recon planes to return immediately. Two of them have more sophisticated equipment and can work in the dark. Hopefully, you can locate the raft and direct the others to it so we can keep it under surveillance until the rescue ship and aircraft arrive in the area."

"Admiral Strange has ordered the *Alabama* and the *Cobb* to detach itself from the fleet and travel at flank speed for the rest of today and throughout the night in order to get within range of the raft's last known location. If you can locate the raft, then the *Alabama* and the *Cobb* will know where to go in order to find it."

"There is a packet for the pilots and crew for your review. Our last known location for the raft was that it was in delta sector of Quadrant 3BK19. However, we will film all of quadrant 3BK19 in order to be sure. Do we have any questions?"

One of the crew stated factitiously, "Who are we looking for the admiral's girlfriend? Seems to be a lot of ships and airplanes to find one raft."

Commander Spencer did not reply. Instead, he pulled out a photo that had been enlarged. He faced the photo toward the group and stated, "This is who you are attempting to rescue."

The photo was of a sad little girl looking up at the sky. There were no further questions.

CHAPTER 13

Sara Housley

Sara Housley was sitting at her news desk. She was a news show producer for WNEX television and radio in Des Moines, Iowa. Her present task was to go over news items for the news day. She was in the process of editing a news story for the evening news when her e-mail icon started to flash indicating that she had an e-mail waiting. A little irritated at being interrupted, she paused to pull up the e-mail.

She looked at the heading on the e-mail and saw that it had come from a public affairs unit at the Pentagon. Attached to the e-mail was a photo. Sara read the message and downloaded the photo. After looking at the photo, she immediately went to contact her station manager.

WNEX television and radio interrupted its regular broadcast for a special bulletin within a few short minutes. The bulletin read:

"We interrupt this regular broadcast to bring you a special news bulletin. This evening, a life and death drama is unfolding in the South Pacific to save the life of a little girl and her parents. Involved is a United States naval task force that is in a race against time with a typhoon force storm. The little girl is in a life raft adrift on a vast ocean with a fierce storm bearing down on her and her family. If the little girl is not rescued by late afternoon tomorrow Honolulu time, the storm will pass through the area destroying the life raft, the little girl, and her parents.

The Pentagon public information office has confirmed that a rescue operation has been launched by a Task Force Tango which is on maneuvers in the South Pacific.

This story has an unusual beginning. Details that have become available indicates that the rescue effort began when an airline passenger, who is believed to be a law enforcement official, spotted what appeared to be an SOS signal. The sighting was relayed by the airline to the United States Coast Guard, Honolulu.

The Honolulu Coast Guard sent out a routine inquiry to all stations on the West Coast of the United States and Mexico asking if any station had a report of any missing or overdue boats.

Within a couple of hours of sending that message, the Coast Guard received a report from a Mexican communications center indicating they had picked up a garbled message from an unidentified boat that may have been sinking. That transmission was received about a month ago. A local inquiry was made by Mexican authorities, but they were not able to confirm the transmission or determine its origin.

Yesterday, the Coast Guard in Seattle received a report of an overdue boat named the *Nadia Marie* based out of Seattle. The boat is owned by a John and Julie Schwartz of Seattle.

Mexican Customs officials in Ensenada, Mexico, confirm that the *Nadia Marie* was there in June and left after a four-day stay. She has not rather been heard from since nor did the boat report into Honolulu Customs as required.

A satellite photo has surfaced showing a little girl sitting in a life raft afloat on the ocean. The photo is on your screen as we speak.

Authorities are checking with the person who filed the original missing report to ascertain whether the photo is a photo of Nadia Marie Schwartz, the daughter of the owner of the *Nadia Marie*. We will keep you updated as this story progresses. Back to our regular broadcast."

Sara would never know that a high school admirer had just made her famous.

CHAPTER 14

The President

President Greg Weedin had a tough day. The Palestinians and Israelis were at it. Israel had assassinated a rather high-ranking Palestinian in Cairo Egypt. Palestine pointed its fingers at Israel. Israel denied involvement, but everyone knew that the Israelis hated this guy. He had been involved in several vicious attacks on Israel.

On the home front, the railroad workers went on strike. Students at Berkeley were on a rampage over some idiotic communist cause that no one but the students involved understood or even cared about.

The first lady was mad at him because he had skipped dinner in order to go over some reports and his daughter Evelyn was coming down with a cold. Just as the president was finishing up with reading the reports an aide came in and said, "Mr. President, you might want to look at this."

The aide went over and turned on one of the cable news channels. The announcer was just repeating a bulletin they had just broadcast. "We are attempting to contact the Pentagon to confirm the story that has been broadcast by WNEX television from Des Moines, Iowa. Again, we are being told that a United States Naval Task Force is racing to save the lives of a little girl and her parents who are adrift on the Pacific Ocean in a life raft after their boat sank. What has complicated this rescue is that a typhoon force storm is moving through the area where the little girl and her family are adrift. If the navy does not reach the little girl and her parents in time, they most assuredly will be killed by the storm. We will update you as we get more details on this developing story."

The aide looked at the president and stated, "Mr. President, you might want to familiarize yourself with this incident. I understand from the switchboard that we are starting to receive numerous calls, which is unusual for this time of night. When I last looked, we were starting to get hundreds of e-mails as well."

President Weedin thanked the aide. He then picked up the phone. When the operator came on the line, he directed the operator to connect him with the Pentagon Operations Center.

Brig. Gen. Al Swift had just arrived at the operations center in the Pentagon for his usual shift. He was waiting for an aide to update him on the day's events when a lieutenant knocked on his office door. General Swift did not look up from his desk. He just stated, "Enter."

The lieutenant approached, saluted, and then stated, "Sir, you have a call holding. It is the White House." The lieutenant then turned and left.

General Swift picked up the phone and identified himself. A voice on the other end identified herself as a White House operator and asked the general to stand by for a call from the president.

General Swift let out a deep breath. He was out all day taking part in a bike-a-thon; the last thing he needed was to have to talk to some politician.

President Weedin came on the line shortly. He asked, "General Swift, can you give me an update on the rescue operation in the South Pacific?"

The general had just arrived and did not have any ready details. He said, "Mr. President, I have just arrived and have not been briefed on today's events. It will take me a minute to get the information. Do you want to hold or can I call you back? I can e-mail you the information if you want."

President Weedin replied, "I don't want an e-mail. I want you to call me personally with the information."

"Yes, Sir, Mr. President," said General Swift. "Give me a minute, and I will call you back."

Within minutes, General Swift called back. When the president picked up the phone, General Swift greeted him and stated, "Mr. President, I have the information on the rescue effort you asked for."

"Thank you, General, go ahead and tell me what you have," said the president.

"Well, Sir, our information is that the Coast Guard received a complaint from an airline that an SOS signal had been seen by a passenger. That passenger was a sheriff on vacation from his office in Lewiston Idaho."

Once the Coast Guard got the report, they sent out a routine inquiry to stations along the West Coasts of the United States and Mexico. In Seattle, a woman reported a boat named the *Nadia Marie* missing two days ago.

Mexican Customs in Ensenada confirmed that the *Nadia Marie* had been in their port for a couple of days, then left for Honolulu. One Mexican communications center located in Baja reported a garbled transmission from a boat that was sinking.

That boat, the *Nadia Marie*, according to the Coast Guard, is the same boat that sent out a Mayday message a little over two weeks ago. Apparently, the Coast Guard was able to filter the transmission received by the Mexican communications center enough to identify the boat.

A photo has been sent to the CINCPAC operations center advising that it was taken by a weather satellite and shows a little girl sitting in a life raft looking skyward. We have a copy of that message which shows that it originated from the White House Situation Room by authority of the Joint Chiefs of Staff. The individual sending the information is code-named "Martha."

President Weedin thanked General Swift and hung up. General Swift wondered why the president was calling him for information.

CHAPTER 15

The Situation Room

President Weedin recognized the code Martha and wondered why they were involved in this event. He decided to go to the situation room to learn more. When President Weedin got to the situation room, a minimum staff was present. It was so dead that one young Marine was doing a crossword puzzle. President Weedin's approach startled the Marine. As he bolted to attention, the Marine knocked over a cup of coffee. The Marine was mortified. He was sure that his career just came to an end, and he would be drummed from the Marine Corps.

President Weedin looked at the young man and said, "You might want to clean that mess up, and while you are at it, have the duty officer report to me in my office immediately."

The Marine saluted and replied, "Yes, Sir." He then hurried across the room to alert the duty officer that the president was in the center. President Weedin went to an office that was set aside for his use whenever he was in the situation room. Presently, the duty officer, Colonel Sharp, appeared and saluted the president. President Weedin returned the salute, then ordered Colonel Sharp to connect him with the task force in the South Pacific that was involved in the rescue of the little girl and her family in the photo. Colonel Sharp saluted, then left to have the communications people contact Admiral Strange, the commander of Task Force Tango.

Within seconds, the room came to life. Keyboards started clicking, conference room lights came on, and video screens came alive. Colonel Sharp came back to the president's office and advised him that the link to Task Force Tango was activated. The president turned to a screen in his office and pushed a button. Admiral Strange appeared on the screen.

Admiral Strange started the conversation by stating, "Good evening, Mr. President."

President Weedin dispensed with the niceties and got right to the point. He said, "Admiral Strange, what is the status of the rescue effort concerning the little girl and her family?"

"At this moment, Mr. President, we have started moving in the general direction of the last coordinates given to us by the airline and a weather satellite photo. We do have a better confirmation of the location of the life raft due to the weather satellite photo taken of the area this morning Honolulu time. Based on the satellite information, we have dispatched two of our fastest ships, the light cruiser *Alabama* and the destroyer escort *Cobb* ahead of the fleet to make the rescue if the raft is located."

"I have sent out a reconnaissance plane to photograph the area and confirm the satellite information on the location of the raft. That plane is on its way back to the fleet as we speak. We should have the results of the recon flight within a couple of hours."

"I had three other recon planes out on a search mission looking for our counterpart in the training mission. Those planes have been recalled and are being readied for the search as soon as the original recon data are processed and analyzed."

"The three recon planes that we are getting ready on the flight line have sophisticated equipment that can see in the dark. Once we locate the raft, we will set up patrol shifts and have the planes stay with the raft until help can arrive."

"Timing on this mission will be very important. We must be able to go directly to the location of the life raft and make the rescue with minimum searching. Weather conditions will be deteriorating as the storm approaches. If the weather worsens, we run the risk of the life raft being swamped and the occupants drowned."

President Weedin said, "Thank you, Admiral. Keep us advised on your progress. Rest assured from me that you can have any means necessary to bring that little girl and her family home."

Admiral Strange acknowledged and signed off. Just as the president signed off, his cell phone started buzzing. He reached into his pocket and pulled out a secure phone. There was a text message that read:

"Check the blue box." That message meant to go to a safe located in the situation room presidential office and open the safe. There would be a laptop computer there. He could then communicate with the staff at "Martha" located in Seneca New York.

The president went to the safe and opened it. He took out a blue case and opened it. Inside was a laptop computer. The president typed a code into the computer and waited for a reply. The reply came almost immediately. It read: "Operation, "See All" is progressing better than expected. There are two Chinese and one Russian sub approaching Task Force Tango. Martha is able to track them without any problem. One of the Chinese subs, the *Wang Su,* will be traveling through the area near the life raft belonging to the *Nadia Marie.* The life raft itself is located in Quadrant 3BK19 in sector DF9Z8. There are three souls aboard."

The president acknowledged the message and signed off. He made a mental note to take action against the individuals who were so blatantly manipulating this event. As the president started to leave the situation room, he approached Colonel Sharp and said, "Colonel, I am going back to the Oval Office. Keep me updated on any news about the rescue. I will be in the office for about another hour, then I am going to bed. Have a report ready for me tomorrow morning when I get up."

"Also send a message to Admiral Strange instructing him to search Quadrant 3BK19 sector DF9Z8 for the life raft."

"Yes, Sir, Mr. President," said Colonel Sharp.

The president left the situation room to return to the Oval Office.

CHAPTER 16

The Reaction

Bedlam is probably the best word to describe what President Weedin encountered when he arrived back at his office. Staffers were on the phone, the phones were ringing constantly, and his press secretary had arrived just as the president came onto the floor.

"What's going on?" asked the president.

His press secretary replied, "The story about the little girl being rescued in the South Pacific has hit all the networks. We are starting to get inquires from around the world. The White House switchboard has lit up. The Pentagon public information section is being deluged with phone calls and e-mails. Public concern for this little girl has gone off the charts. Ninety five percent of the incoming calls are from concerned voters who want us to make sure that the girl in the photo is rescued.

"A news station in Seattle has reported that the photo has been confirmed by the nanny, who made the report to the Coast Guard, is the picture of a Nadia Marie Schwartz, the daughter of John C. Schwartz, a local businessman and state legislator, and his wife Julie A. Schwartz, a prominent businesswoman."

"Everyone who is remotely connected to the family has gotten into the act. News stations are interviewing everyone they can find with any information including friends, neighbors, and even a niece from Sioux Falls South Dakota."

"We now have a report that a Mexican commander from a Mexican communications station in Baja California has released a copy of the SOS transmission believed to have been sent by Julie Schwartz as the boat was about to sink."

"We have a major incident on our hands three months before the election."

All President Weedin could say was, "Thank you, keep me posted if anything major develops. I am going to try and get some sleep. I suspect that tomorrow will be a busy day."

The president was stunned by the attention this whole incident was getting.

CHAPTER 17

The Sighting

Vulcan flight commanded by Commander Harris arrived back from their mission just as the sun began to set. Their photo discs were immediately taken by an analyst to be processed. Commander Harris went immediately to the flight operations center where Commander Spencer was waiting to debrief the crew.

Within minutes, the reconnaissance report was transmitted to Admiral Strange. The recon video clearly showed a life raft afloat with three people aboard. Admiral Strange had the information transmitted to CINCPAC, the Pentagon, and the White House Situation Room as ordered.

Admiral Strange then ordered that his recon planes set up a round-the-clock surveillance on the life raft. In this electronic age, it is not possible to keep a secret long. Most ships in the navy can tune into international broadcasts. Some of the larger ships can access satellite television. Information was slow in coming, but the details of their altered mission were soon known throughout the fleet.

It didn't take long for the sailors of the fleet to figure out that the TV and radio reports were true. They knew something was afoot when the fleet suddenly changed course.

Then the *Alabama* and *Cobb* detached themselves from the fleet and left at high speed. The fleet seemed to be headed in the same direction. The TV and radio reports confirmed their suspicions. Everyone waited for the reconnaissance plane to report. There was little time between the time the plane landed before the fleet knew of the sighting. They also knew that there was a monster bearing down on that little girl and her families. Many who had families of their own said a silent prayer for her safety. The fleet *Chaplin* posted a prayer; it read:

> *"Almighty God, we thy poor and humble servants beseech thee to stay this mighty wind. Stay its progress and protect this innocent child and her family. Give us speed and fair weather to reach this family. Send thy spirit, oh Lord, to comfort and protect little Nadia Marie and her parents until our fleet can arrive to help and protect her."*

All reconnaissance planes were now fueled and actively engaged in the rescue attempt. Each plane would fly overhead until relieved by another.

There was a constant stream of information between the planes and the fleet. Newer infrared equipment was used to photograph the raft and send images back through a military satellite system. The infrared photos showed the three people aboard the raft.

The thermal imaging equipment on the planes was so accurate that the individual body temperatures of the persons on the raft were recorded. Thermal imaging showed their body temperatures ranged from normal to slightly higher than the temperature of the human body.

One of the images in particular showed a much higher temperature than the normal human temperature.

CHAPTER 18

The Dream

After a few days, John Schwartz had lapsed into a semiconscious state. Sometimes he would moan and talk in his sleep. He had deliberately given part of his food and water ration to his wife and child. The lack of food and water and his head injury was taking its toll on his body.

Julie was not doing much better. She too had given more to Nadia in the hopes that a rescue would come. She had begun to drift in and out of consciousness. When she could, she would hold Nadia and try to sing to her. The lack of water was making it more difficult to even talk. When she cried, they were dry tears. She had reached an advanced stage of dehydration along with her husband.

Julie saw the sun coming up and knew that she would not have many more sunrises. She drifted off but was awakened by Nadia pleading with her.

"Mommy, don't die, please. The men are coming to get us!"

Julie struggled to sit up. A faint glimmer of hope had appeared in her consciousness. She asked, "What… men?"

Nadia replied, "The men in the planes were here last night. The pirates are coming to save us."

Julie began to shed dry tears. Her daughter was hallucinating. She pulled Nadia close and began to face another day. She could not bear the thought of her daughter dying alone.

CHAPTER 19

The Breakdown

It was not a message that one would like to receive at breakfast. It was simple and to the point.

"Commander *USS Alabama* to Tango Commander: We have experienced a bearing failure on one of our drive shafts which has caused us to slow. At our present knots, we will not be able to conclude the rescue mission assigned this vessel for at least an additional five hours."

The commander of the *Alabama* was simply stating that the rescue would not be in time to save the Schwartz family. Admiral Strange had an aide send the sad news to CINCPAC, the situation room and the Pentagon. The message read:

"*USS Alabama* has had a mechanical failure which has caused a slowing of speed. At her present rate of speed, she will not be able to effect the rescue of the Schwartz family in time."

In Washington, President Weedin was having lunch when he got the news. It was one of the few times that he had ever lost his temper, but this time, he lost control. In a loud angry voice he stated, "We have the largest most formidable navy in the world, and we can't rescue a little girl! I'll be damned!"

The president lapsed into silence in order to regain his composure. Everyone around him heard the cell phone break the silence as they waited for the president to regain his composure.

The message on the phone was short. It read: "Contact Martha." "Damn them," the president thought. "These spooks got me into this mess, and I am going to get even with the individual who leaked that photo to some bimbo in Des Moines, Iowa."

President Weedin stood up and stated, "Excuse me. I have a matter I need to attend to."

The president went directly to the situation room. Without saying a word, he went into the office assigned him and took out the blue case from the safe. He entered his code into the computer and awaited a reply. The message came quickly. It read:

"The Chinese submarine named the *Wang Su* will be passing through the 3BK19 quadrant around 1600 hours. It can make the rescue if you request it."

President Weedin acknowledged the message and signed off. He was thinking about the message and its consequences. To ask a foreign government, especially the Chinese, to rescue the Schwartz family would be political suicide. Once the fact was known that the Chinese made the rescue, his enemies would have a public relations field day.

He had to admit that Martha was working better than he had expected. Still he was going to make life miserable for the individuals who got him into this mess. President Weedin returned to the Oval Office. He went over and turned on a TV to listen to the news. Just as he sat down, his daughter, Evelyn, came in and sat on his lap. The president turned up the volume on the TV with his remote. A special news broadcast was just being aired.

> "We have learned from the Pentagon that the ship, the USS Alabama, that was assigned to rescue the Schwartz family has suffered a mechanical failure. As you recall, this is the ship along with its support ship the USS Cobb that was assigned to rescue little Nadia Marie Schwartz and her family from a deadly typhoon approaching their tiny raft afloat on a vast Pacific Ocean.
>
> Sources at the Pentagon tell us that the USS Cobb, the Alabama support ship initially slowed to assist the Alabama. The Cobb is now traveling at top speed to rescue Nadia Marie and her family from certain death. Our Pentagon sources say that the captain and crew of the Cobb volunteered to continue on into the deadly storm to try and rescue little Nadia and her family even though such an attempt would place the Cobb and crew in grave danger.
>
> Once the Cobb reaches the area, it could be guided to the raft by reconnaissance planes who have maintained a constant vigil over the raft throughout the night. However, the weather service indicates that the speed of the hurricane has picked up further limiting the time to rescue Nadia and her family.

At this point, any rescue attempt would be in high seas placing rescuers and rescued in jeopardy.

People from all over the world are saying prayers for Nadia and her family. In Rome, the pope is holding a special vigil.

We will keep you informed on this story as it continues."

President Weedin looked down at his daughter. There were tears running down her cheeks. In a childlike voice, she looked at the president and stated, "Daddy, can't you save the little girl?"

"I'll try," responded the president. "Now, you and I will go and find Mommy. Daddy has lots of work to do."

After the president took his daughter to their living quarters in the White House, he returned to the Oval Office and picked up the phone.

CHAPTER 20

The Cancellation

President Weedin returned to the situation room. The evening shift had gone home. A brigadier general was present and in command. President Weedin ignored them all initially. Instead, he had the communications section pull up a grid map of the area where the life raft was located. He then started to issue orders to the staff.

His first order was to Admiral Strange of Task Force Tango. It read:

"Presidential Authorization—1WH986. Recall the rescue ships Alabama and Cobb, risk to men and ships is too great. Redirect the Alabama and Cobb to grid 4WY834DB and have them stand by in that location."

Word of the failure of the rescue attempt and the presidential order spread throughout the fleet. Even some of the tough old senior petty officers had tears in their eyes.

Reconnaissance planes sent to monitor the raft were reporting low visibility and high winds starting to develop. A marker buoy was placed near the raft. The last recon plane then headed for the carrier. There was no hope left for the Schwartz family.

Admiral Strange had his fleet change course to intercept the *Alabama* and *Cobb* in grid 4WY834DB. There, the fleet could rendezvous with the two ships, avoid the storm, and continue its training mission.

The admiral was puzzled by the presidential order. It made no sense not to have the two ships just return to the fleet.

CHAPTER 21

The Pirates

Julie Schwartz had been drifting in and out of consciousness. In one of her lucid moments, she noticed that the wind had increased. The sun had disappeared behind what looked like rain clouds. She took the tarp to try and trap some rain water if it did rain, but a sudden wind jerked the tarp away. Julie struggled to try and catch the tarp, but she was too weak. Nadia tried to help her, but the wind gust was too strong, and the tarp blew away.

Julie sank down in despair. Without the tarp to catch the water, they would continue to dehydrate and die. There would be no shelter from the sun. If dehydration did not kill them, then the blistering sun would.

Nadia tried to comfort her mother to no avail. Nadia told Julie about the planes, and how they came and left a blinking light to guide the pirates who were coming to save them. Nadia's story of pirates to the rescue was too much to take. Julie was too exhausted and sick. Her depression worsened when Nadia told her about the pirates. She knew that death was near for both of them.

Had Julie arose and looked around, she could have easily seen the strobe light blinking a hundred yards off her stern. Julie had been sailing long enough to know that the clouds overhead signaled that a storm was coming. She knew that if the storm was severe enough, it would swamp the life raft, and they would all drown. Perhaps it would be more merciful if they all drowned than face the terrible heat and dehydration that awaited them. In utter despair and exhaustion, Julie gave up and collapsed.

Through a fog of exhaustion, Julie heard a humming sound that got louder and louder. She could feel the boat moving up and down with the swells caused by the wind. Maybe the humming sound was a final wave that would engulf them and end their suffering. It would be merciful.

Through blurred vision, Julie saw a face, then another, and another.

They were oriental faces and the persons spoke gibberish.

"How ironic," Julie thought, "these probably were pirates who had come to steal their possessions and leave them to die." Maybe it was Nadia's pirates who had come to take them to a land of make-believe where pirates, princesses, and dragons lived. Then she passed out.

Nadia had been a brave little girl. When her dad was injured on the boat, she had gotten the first aid kit to help bandage his wound. She had even managed to keep the boat on an even keel by holding fast to the boat's steering wheel while her mother tended to her father and secured the mast boom. Day after day, she played quietly and did not complain. A food wrapper became a blanket for her make-believe playmates. She used her imagination to create other toys and invisible friends.

When a plane flew over far up in the sky, she would take out an emergency signal mirror she had found in the emergency kit and signal the plane. This mirror had a crank that would charge up the mirror battery. A very intense and bright light would flash when Nadia pushed a button. One time, Nadia looked directly at the light to see if it was working. The flash from the light blinded her for a couple of minutes. Nadia decided to never try that again. Above all else, she never gave up hope.

She helped her mother tend to her father after he became semiconscious. Sometimes she would help her mother force her father to drink and eat. When her mother began to be disoriented and sleep a lot, she would make her mother eat and drink. Her mother would hold her and sing to her when she could.

One night, Nadia had a dream that men in planes were searching for them. They were in black planes that flew through the sky and could not be seen. They were mysterious planes that flew like ghosts unseen and unheard. Then she dreamt that pirates dressed in funny clothes and speaking an unknown language were coming to save her and her parents.

After the tarp blew away, she tried to tell her mother about the planes and the pirates to give her support. Her mother had just held her closer, then seemed to pass out. She was awake in the afternoon when the plane had flown over and dropped the blinking light. Nadia tried to awaken her mother to tell her, but her mother had only mumbled and went back to sleep.

Nadia watched as the sky turned gray and the swells got bigger. She pretended that she was on a roller coaster at the Seattle Center. When she saw the pirates coming in their small yellow boat, she knew them. She could see their ship in the distance. She thought it odd that the ship did not have sails like a pirate ship. She didn't care. These were the pirates in her dream. When the first pirate reached her, she grabbed him by the neck and squeezed as hard as she could. This was her pirate.

CHAPTER 22

The Rendezvous

Captain Marvin Goetz was exhausted. He had spent all night fixing the mechanical problem with his ship. His reputation was on the line and so was the reputation of the ship. He had earned a reputation as a can-do commander. This whole problem had made him livid. A factory defect had caused the bearing to fail. Now he was unable to save a little girl and her family while the whole world watched.

Then came the message from Admiral Strange to call off his attempt to reach the little girl. Along with the cancellation of the mission was a message that made no sense. He was directed to go to grid 4WY834DB and stand by. Why didn't the admiral just order him to report back to the fleet?

Captain Goetz had his XO assume command. He was tired and needed to take a nap before they arrived on station in grid 4WY834DB. The order did not have any instructions other than to report that they had arrived on station. He instructed the XO to send a message to Admiral Strange when they arrived.

As instructed, the XO sent the message to Admiral Strange once they arrived on station. Within minutes, a confirmation message did not come from Admiral Strange; it came from the White House Situation Room. It too was a brief message. It read:

> *"Your message received that you have arrived at grid 4WY834DB. You are to stand by for further instructions. Confirmation 1WH986A."*

The Rescue of the Nadia Marie

The XO was taken aback. This was a message direct from the White House Situation Room. He immediately sent an ensign to wake the captain up and alert him to the message and their arrival on station.

A second message from the White House Situation Room was sent to Admiral Strange at Task Force Tango with copies to the *Alabama* and *Cobb*. It read:

> *"Authorization code 1WH987. To Admiral Strange Task Force Tango. You are ordered to alter your course and not enter grid 4WY834DB. You are to proceed to grid 3WY835BE and stand by for further orders."*

Admiral Strange sent an acknowledgement to the message. He noted that these messages were bypassing CINCPAC and the normal chain of command. It appeared that the president was directing his fleet's every move.

Captain Goetz on the *Alabama* received the report from his XO, then gave instructions to his XO to immediately notify him of any change in status. He then went back to his quarters again to try and get a catnap. He didn't know it, but his nap was not to last long.

To the captain, it seemed that he had just closed his eyes when a lieutenant assigned to the communications center knocked on his door. Captain Goetz bid the lieutenant to enter. The lieutenant saluted and stated, "Sir, you have an Alpha 1 message from the president of the United States."

The captain took the message and thanked the lieutenant. The lieutenant saluted and left.

Captain Goetz was to later say that the message he received was the most astounding message he had received in his career. It read:

> *"Authorization Alpha 1WH988. You are to proceed with the USS Cobb to point F41G82. There, you will meet the People's Liberation Army naval vessel the Wang Su. You will extend all courtesies to PLA Shang Xiao Chen Wei and his crew. You are ordered to take aboard your vessel and provide medical attention to three American citizens believed to be two adults and one child. You are to evacuate these citizens to a proper medical facility as soon as possible. You are ordered to express the thanks and gratitude of myself and our nation to PLA*

> *Hai Jun Shang Xiao Chen Wei and his crew. As soon as you accomplish this mission, you are to make a report directly to this office. President Greg Weedin."*

"This whole message does not make sense," thinks Captain Goetz. There are no reports of a Chinese navy submarine in the area. He decided that there was not going to be any nap for him, so he headed for the bridge.

When the captain arrived on the bridge, he ordered the XO to set a course for point F41G82 as ordered. He then had a message sent to the *Cobb* directing them to follow the *Alabama* and to stand by if needed. It took about two hours for the *Alabama* and *Cobb* to reach the designated point. There was no other vessel in the area. The two vessels slowed and began to sail in a holding pattern. About another two hours, a lookout reported a submarine surfacing off the port bow of the *Alabama*.

At the same time, sonar reported an unidentified submarine surfacing 123 degrees off the port bow. Captain Goetz was stunned. His reaction was to question how that Chinese wang ba got there without being detected.

Aboard the *USS Cobb* the XO sounded battle stations. Their captain had to order the crew to stand down. Once the shock wore off that there was a Chinese submarine sitting off the port bow of the *Alabama,* Captain Goetz started reacting. He had the signalman on the bridge establish contact with the sub. That was done in short order.

Captain Chen Wei of the *Wang Su* sent a message to the *Alabama* which read:

> *"Commander of the USS Alabama—Greetings from the People's Liberation Army Naval Ship the Wang Su Captain Chen Wei commanding. We have aboard our vessel three American citizens that we have rescued from a life raft. We have been instructed to turn these people over to you. How do you wish to proceed?"*

Captain Goetz had his communications officer send a message to the Chinese submarine that read:

> "It is probably safer that we send our helicopter over to the aft section of your vessel and take the three aboard from there. Light up your aft section so the helicopter can see where to land. We have stretchers that we can transfer the people to if they cannot walk. Maintain our present parallel course at ten knots until the transfer is made."

Captain Goetz then had the helipad and his ship lit up so the Chinese captain could plainly see his ship. Within a couple of minutes, the lights on the *Wang Su* lit up the aft section of the vessel.

A helicopter was dispatched to the submarine. Within minutes, two persons were transferred into the helicopter. The third person, a little girl, became hysterical and refused to leave without a Chinese Er Ji Shi Guan named Kai Che. He is the equivalent of a pharmacist mate in the US Navy.

In the few hours that Nadia spent with Seaman Kai Che, she developed a strong bond with him. Nadia referred to him as her pirate. Nadia's reaction was so strong to leaving the seaman that Captain Goetz felt that any forced separation of the two might harm the little girl mentally. Captain Goetz finally asked permission from Captain Chen Wei if the seaman could accompany the Schwartz family with the understanding that he would be returned to the Chinese navy through their embassy in Honolulu. Reluctantly, Captain Wei gave his consent. That calmed Nadia down, and she got onto the helicopter with her pirate Kai Che.

After the rescue was complete, Captain Goetz had a case of champagne sent to Captain Chen Wei along with a letter from Captain Goetz expressing the gratitude of the American people for the assistance given in rescuing the three American citizens.

Once the transfer was complete, the *Alabama* signaled the *Wang Su*. Captain Chen Wei acknowledged the message. Silently the *Wang Su* submerged back into the depths of the ocean from which it came. Within minutes, the *Alabama* sonar lost contact with the sub. It was as if it was never there.

Once aboard the *Alabama*, the three, two adults and a child, were sent to sickbay for treatment. Sickbay confirmed that the three were John and Julie Schwartz and their daughter Nadia from Seattle, Washington.

Captain Goetz sent a message as ordered to the White House Situation Room and to Admiral Strange, the task force commander. It read:

"Have rendezvoused with the Chinese naval submarine, the Wang Su. We have aboard three American citizens identified as John Schwartz, Julie Schwartz, and their daughter Nadia Marie Schwartz of Seattle, Washington. Accompanying the Schwartz family is a Chinese petty officer named Kai Che.

The child Nadia had become hysterical and refused to leave the Chinese sailor. I felt that it was best to have the sailor accompany Nadia rather than risk permanent mental damage to the child. Captain Chen Wei gave his consent with the understanding that we would return the sailor through the Chinese Consulate in Honolulu.

Julie Schwartz is severely dehydrated but is responding to treatment. Her vital signs are stable. She is still in a semiconscious state.

Nadia Schwartz is in a state of mild shock but is responding to treatment. She is able to talk and sit up.

John Schwartz is in a comatose state. He is dehydrated, has a head injury, and possibly a brain hemorrhage. He is stable but critical and will require medical attention that is not available on this vessel.

We are en route to grid 3WY835BE to meet Task Force Tango and transfer our civilians."

CHAPTER 23

The Fleet

It was a beautiful sunrise as the helicopter lifted off the deck of the *Alabama*. The deadly storm had been skirted. Aboard the helicopter were Nadia, her mother, her dad, and her pirate Kai Che. As the group left the *Alabama* behind, another sight came into view—a flotilla of ships were sailing just over the horizon. There were small ships and medium ships all surrounding a huge ship with airplanes on its deck.

Nadia realized that these were the ships in her dream. She snuggled up to Kai Che, her pirate, and for the first time, she began to cry.

Julie was sedated but was somewhat alert to her surroundings. As the helicopter neared the huge carrier, she could see lights flashing from ships and heard foghorns bellowing out a welcome.

When the copter landed on the deck of the carrier, there were sailors lining up on the flight deck cheering and clapping. Kai Che was taken aback by it all. He was treated as a hero. He was assigned an officer who spoke Mandarin to assist him while he was aboard. Everywhere he went, sailors would stop to shake his hand or slap him on the back. Some of the sailors took photos of Kai Che and themselves. The pictures soon made their way to the Internet. Kai Che became known worldwide through the Internet. Kai Che was oblivious to the sudden fame. He did not have access to the Internet and would not know for some time the extent of the publicity and acclaim he was getting.

One group of sailors taught him how to high-five. Kai Che didn't quite understand the gesture but soon adapted to its use. Mostly he tried to stay with Nadia and her family. Kai Che kept watch over Nadia and her parents. Nadia would climb up onto Kai Che's lap and take short naps. When Julie would come to, he would hold her hand and talk to her. Julie did not understand a word he said, but she sensed that he cared and was taking care of her.

All of the doctors and nurses involved in the care of the Schwartz family were amazed at the bond between Kai Che and his charges. It was decided to let him stay with the family since they seemed to respond to him so well, especially the little girl. When it came time to evacuate the family and Kai Che, the doctors and nurses gave Kai Che a small plaque expressing their gratitude for his excellent care and concern for the Schwartz family.

When the family was put aboard the plane, there was a small honor guard and sailors who lined the way to the entrance of the plane. Admiral Strange was there and gave a salute as the plane started down the takeoff runway of the carrier. There was hardly a dry eye in the crowd.

Once in Honolulu, the hospital was flooded with reporters from all over the world trying to get a picture of the Schwartz family and Nadia's pirate. Upon arrival at the hospital, Kai Che was met by a member of the Chinese consulate. To his surprise, his mother and father were there with the consulate official.

Even Kai Che's mother and father did not fully understand what was happening. Their first indication that something was afoot was when a shiny new sedan pulled up in front of their small laundry business, and a man in an expensive suit got out and came inside the shop. This generally meant government trouble. They were surprised when they were instructed to go with the official and get on an airplane to meet their son in some place called Hawaii, which was part of the United States. They were told that their son was a hero of the state.

Nadia's aunt, Sharon Mott, from Sioux Falls, South Dakota, was waiting for them. Nadia had responded quite well to the medical treatment aboard ship, so she was turned over to her aunt. Both attended the farewell of Kai Che when a special plane from the Chinese prime minister was flown in to take him and his parents home. Nadia presented Kai Che with a gold wristwatch. On the back was an inscription that read: "You will be in my heart forever, Nadia."

CHAPTER 24

The Reckoning

Admiral Strange was a fourth-generation seaman. His family had a proud sea tradition going back over a hundred years. This naval tradition had started with his great-grandfather. His great-great-grandfather had been a bartender in the old west town of Dodge City, Kansas, and never left dry land.

He had entered the navy out of high school. As an enlisted man, Strange excelled. Because of his proficiency, he was given the opportunity to attend the Naval Academy. He was the first in his family to attend the academy. Both his father and grandfather had retired as master chiefs.

His two sons had decided not to pursue a naval career, but his first grandson was to start the Naval Academy in the fall. The admiral had taught naval tactics in the Naval Academy and hoped to return to teach his grandson before he retired.

It was obvious that it did not take an entire task force to rescue people in a life raft; however, to outsmart his second in command, Admiral Harney, and his bravo aggressor force, Admiral Strange would have to take advantage of the whole operation.

Neither was Admiral Strange ignorant of modern computers and technology. He had on his ship young sailors, one of which was some sort of video game wizard that had come up with an innovative way to circumvent the mission rules of not using military satellites to seek out and track their adversaries, Bravo Group, led by Rear Admiral Harney. The plan was simple: use Google Earth to locate the adversary. There would be no violation of mission rules. Of course, Admiral Strange knew that if he was using Google Earth, then Admiral Harney had probably figured it out as well. He had to come up with some way of escaping the satellite's eyes.

With the storm approaching and a rescue operation ongoing, it provided the admiral with the perfect opportunity. He let all the ships in his command maintain television and radio satellite contact in order to allow the Bravo force to detect the electronic signature. When the rescue mission was completed, the admiral had all electronic communications blacked out. He simply disappeared off the radar.

Admiral Harney came from a family of mixed military and political ancestors. He was a good tactician and had graduated at the top of his class in the Naval Academy. After he graduated from the Academy, he was assigned to various positions that were well placed to advance his career. His father was a United States Senator and retired admiral. He made sure that his son got the best assignments and shepherded his career. In spite of this obvious influence, Admiral Harney studied hard and advanced in rank. Being placed under Admiral Strange was another stepping stone in his career. He not only got command experience but also, he was being taught by one of the best tacticians in the navy. Admiral Strange was ready to retire that meant his next star would be assured as he would be slated to take Admiral Strange's position.

Harney did have one small failing. He had an ego problem. In his quest to be the best, he had become somewhat arrogant. This arrogance was to lead to his comeuppance.

Mission rules stated that Bravo Group would be on station at a designated place within a certain time frame. There was no set rule as to when they could arrive and depart from the designated position. The start of the training mission would begin on a set time schedule. Admiral Harney arrived early and promptly left.

He imposed a complete blackout on his group. Once he felt that he had evaded detection, he allowed one electronic communications seaman to use Google Earth to locate Admiral Strange's group. Once Admiral Strange's group was located, the electronic connection was shut off. Admiral Harney then began to plot his strategy.

All was going as planned for Bravo Group until an unexpected event occurred. Admiral Harney was on the bridge when the intercom buzzed from his communications center. The voice on the other end stated, "Admiral, we have an update on Admiral Strange's position." Admiral Harney replied, "Go ahead."

The communications center caller started his report, "Admiral, we are not sure what is going on. According to Google Earth, Admiral Strange has suddenly altered course. He is headed on a collision course with the approaching typhoon."

Harney was taken aback. Harney thought, "He is not that stupid. He would not put his whole group into jeopardy by taking them into the path of a typhoon. What is he up to?"

Bravo Group kept track of Admiral Strange's group until darkness fell. He seemed to be heading on a set course which would indeed take him and his ships into the path of the typhoon that would pass over him the next afternoon if he continued on his present course.

Early next morning, Bravo Group again established contact with Admiral Strange. He was still on a course headed into the typhoon. Within hours, Admiral Harney was notified that Admiral Strange had altered course and was passing east and parallel in front of the approaching storm. Around midafternoon, the sky became too cloudy and contact was lost.

Admiral Harney had intended to swing wide to the south of Admiral Strange, then attack him from the east as the sun was rising. That would have put his group in a position of having the sun to their backs. It was not much of an edge, but it was an edge.

It was easy to pick up the electronic signature from the fleet. Admiral Strange had turned on the radio and TV system so the crew could watch TV or listen to radio on their off times. Even after the start of the exercise began, Admiral Strange allowed the TV and radio systems to remain on for a short period of time. Admiral Harney thought that was a poor thing to do in this day and age of electronic surveillance. Harney felt this was going to be easy to show his superior how the younger generation dealt with old dinosaurs.

There were transmissions between the fleet and Honolulu for a brief period of time, then the fleet suddenly altered course. Strangely, a cruiser and a destroyer escort support ship to the cruiser detached itself from the fleet and went ahead of the main group.

A small AWACS plane had been sent up to monitor any incoming planes or traffic. The AWACS spotted three recon planes and sent a short message to Bravo Group alerting them to the presence of the planes. Within minutes of coming in radar range of the AWACS and ultimately of Bravo Group, the reconnaissance planes suddenly turned around and headed off in a westerly direction which would take them back to the fleet.

With the oncoming storm, Admiral Harney decided to move his fleet farther to the east of the storm and let it pass by. He maintained strict radio silence. Once Admiral Strange had no chance of detecting his location, Admiral Harney allowed his communications center to monitor the civilian airwaves to pick up any news of the storm. He soon learned of the rescue mission involving Task Force Tango.

News of the rescue attempt caused Admiral Harney to be concerned that the exercise was to be called off. He had his communications center query CINCPAC on the status of the exercise. The reply was immediate. He was to continue the exercise as planned. That was a fatal error. Admiral Strange picked up the electronic signal.

When the storm passed by, Admiral Harney began the task of finding Admiral Strange and his group. If the admiral had used his head, he would have gone to the west of the storm which was moving in a southeasterly direction. That meant the logical place to look for Admiral Strange would be to the west.

Admiral Strange was not a logical commander. He had learned through hard experience that if you did the expected, you would lose. Instead of veering to the west, he moved his task force to the east. This put him on a direct path toward Task Force Bravo for a short while. It also put him into the eastern edge of the storm. Once the admiral had reached the eastern edge of the storm, he turned his ships to the northwest to stay inside the trailing edge of the storm. Admiral Strange maneuvered his task force to the rear of the storm, then followed the tail end of the storm to the southeast which took him to the south of Bravo Group and slightly to the east of the Bravo formation. The storm and low visibility kept his task force from the prying eyes of Google Earth or any reconnaissance aircraft. At one point, his task force passed in front of Task Force Bravo as it proceeded to the southeast with the storm. Once Task Force Tango was well to the south and east of Task Force Bravo, Admiral Strange had his task force turn to the north northeast to come up to the east of Task Force Bravo.

Seaman David Donnelly of the USS Jefferson an aegis class destroyer on picket duty on the eastern flank of Bravo Group was the first to become aware of an anomaly on his radar screen. Two faint blips appeared on his radar screen, then disappeared. A couple of minutes later, the two blips again appeared, then disappeared. When the blips again appeared and then disappeared, Donnelly decided to test his equipment. At first, he tested high altitude reading, then he tested low altitude. Nothing appeared on his screen. He then decided to test his equipment at ground level.

Two blips began to show up on the radar screen. They were faint, then got more pronounced. As best as the seaman could tell there were two planes traveling at an extremely high speed about hundred feet off the ocean surface. He picked up his intercom to alert the bridge. It was too late.

Just as the captain of the Jefferson picked up his intercom, two stealth fighter bombers went by on both sides of his bridge. The two planes were so close that the pilots waved at him as they passed. The planes then accelerated and began to climb. Within seconds, they were out of sight and headed for the center of the battle group.

Admiral Harney had just been alerted to the two bogies when a loud sonic boom rattled the bridge. Then a second sonic boom rattled the bridge again. Two stealth fighter bombers flew across his flight deck. Both of them climbed up and did a barrel roll. Then the two planes came back down and flew across his deck again breaking the sound barrier at midpoint of the flight deck.

A radio transmission from one of the fighter said in a thick southern accent, "Admiral Strange sends his compliments to you boys. The admiral told us to tell y'all to have his champagne ready when you rendezvous for the trip home. You boys have a good day." The two planes then left headed east southeast away from the task force.

CHAPTER 25

The Confirmation

President Weedin had waited up to hear of the news of the rescue. It had been a tiring day. He had to meet with the German ambassador, then the Saudi ambassador. Then he had to go to the press club and give a speech in the evening. Everywhere he went, he had to field questions about the rescue of the Schwartz family.

While he was waiting, President Weedin decided to look over a farm bill that he was being encouraged to sign. An aide came in and interrupted him, "Mr. President, here is the report you were waiting for from the situation room on the Schwartz family rescue." The aide then handed him the report. "While you are at it, sir, you might want to look at the late-night news."

The president acknowledged the aide and asked her to turn on the TV. An announcer was just announcing a news story out of Beijing: "We have just learned from the Xin Hua the Official Chinese News Agency that the Chinese navy has rescued little Nadia Marie Schwartz and her family in the South Pacific. We go now to a broadcast made just a few moments ago."

The news service then cut into the video feed. A young rather stunning Chinese newswoman was reading a statement from the office of the prime minister of China. It read: "We are honored to inform the people of China and the world that the People's Liberation Army Hai Jun has rescued an American girl named Nadia Marie Schwartz and her family from certain death. A Hai Jun submarine named the *Wang Su* and commanded by Shang Xiao Chen Wei and his brave crew rescued the Americans this morning. Our beloved leader Tai Wan Lei dispatched the vessel after learning of the little girl's plight from the

American President Weedin. The American president requested that the prime minister assist when a rescue effort involving two American ships had failed in their attempt to rescue the little girl.

"Our navy is now transporting the little girl and her family to the US Navy so they can receive medical treatment and be reunited with their friends and family in the United States. We will have a more formal statement from the prime minister later on today."

President Weedin swore under his breath. "That hundan will play this to the hilt."

The American announcer continued on, "A rescue attempt in the South Pacific has turned into an extraordinary story. The story had its beginning yesterday when a vacationing county sheriff from Nez Perce County Idaho named Eldon Fogus spotted an SOS signal from his airplane window. Airline personnel did not believe the sheriff initially but agreed to report the incident when Sheriff Fogus identified himself and became insistent that the sighting be reported."

"The airline reported the sighting to the Honolulu Coast Guard, who also reacted skeptically. However, the Coast Guard sent a routine inquiry out to Coast Guard stations along the West Coast and the West Coast of Mexico asking if any station had a report of a missing boat. Within hours, the Coast Guard learned that a boat named the *Nadia Marie* belonging to a John and Julie Schwartz of Seattle, Washington, was overdue."

"A Mexican communications center in Baja California reported that they had intercepted an SOS from a vessel believed to be sinking about three to four weeks ago. The Mexican commander had made an inquiry but neither could find any report of a missing boat nor did any other station in Baja pick up the SOS message. That commander did respond to the Coast Guard inquiry which caused an alert to go out to the West Coast Coast Guard stations."

"About the same time of the Mexican report, the Coast Guard in Seattle notified the Honolulu Coast Guard station that they had received a report of an overdue boat named the *Nadia Marie* headed for Seattle via Ensenada, Mexico, to Honolulu and finally to Seattle."

"Mexican Customs in Ensenada confirmed that the overdue boat the *Nadia Marie* had been in their port in June and had departed for Honolulu."

"One of the problems encountered by the Coast Guard was that the position reported to them by the airline was at the point of no return for aircraft traversing the area. Planes could not search the area nor were there any merchant ships in the area. A naval task force was operating in the area, however. A request was sent to the navy from the Coast Guard asking for their assistance."

"A military weather satellite that was monitoring a storm approaching the area took a picture of a little girl in a life raft in the area where the SOS signal was first reported. That picture was obtained by a small TV station in Des Moines, Iowa, who broadcast the story. As a result of the story and picture, worldwide attention soon focused on the rescue effort to save the little girl and her parents."

"Several hours into the rescue attempt, one of the ships dispatched to the rescue had a mechanical failure that slowed its progress. A second rescue support ship and its captain and crew volunteered to go into the storm at great risk to the ship and men to try and save the little girl and her family. President Weedin who was monitoring the rescue attempt from the White House Situation Room called the ships off due to the extreme danger to ships and crews."

"President Weedin had intelligence information that a Chinese submarine was in the area of the life raft. Disregarding any political repercussions, he called Chinese Prime Minister Lei and asked him to assist in the rescue. It was reported that initially the Chinese premier was hesitant to admit that there was a submarine operating in the area but finally relented when he was convinced of the seriousness of the little girl's plight."

"As you have heard from the Chinese News Agency that Chinese submarine was able to rescue the little girl and her parents."

"We now understand that the family has positively been identified as John and Julie Schwartz and their daughter Nadia Marie of Seattle, Washington. Initial reports are that little Nadia Marie is in a state of shock. Her mother Julie Schwartz is in critical but stable condition. The father John Schwartz is in critical condition."

"A heartwarming story has emerged out of this tragedy. There is a Chinese sailor whose rank is an Er Ji Shi Guan in the Chinese navy which would be like a medic or pharmacist mate in our navy is attending to the Schwartz family. In the few hours that Nadia spent with the seaman, she developed a bond with this seaman who is named Kai Che. When Nadia was about to be transferred from the Chinese vessel to the American vessel, she became hysterical and refused to leave what she termed her *pirate*. Rather than risk mental damage to little Nadia, it was decided to allow the Chinese seaman to accompany Nadia and her family. He is now with the family aboard an American ship."

Seaman Kai Che has emerged as a kind and caring hero of this tragedy.

"Another twist has developed in this story. A captain of a marine biology vessel is being quoted as claiming that the *Nadia Marie* and its owners found and assisted a whale tangled up in a fishing net off the coast of Mexico near Ensenada. We have not confirmed this story, but we will keep you posted as this story develops further."

President Weedin read the dispatches on the rescue and decided to go to bed. To his surprise, his daughter Evelyn was awake and waiting for him. She grabbed her father around the neck and said, "You are the bestest pirate captain ever, Daddy."

CHAPTER 26

The Report

Eyes only report to the director of the Central Intelligence Agency.

"As you know, Task Force Tango had a hidden agenda. It was a training exercise but the hidden goal was to test a new satellite system code-named Martha. That satellite system is not only capable of recording any debris and ships on the ocean within a five hundred mile radius in any weather but also it is capable of detecting anything up to five hundred feet below the ocean surface. This gives us the capability to see anything that moves on or under the ocean."

"The *Nadia Marie* incident gave Task Force Tango the opportunity to test their capabilities at finding a potential threat to the fleet or our nation. I might say that Task Force Tango carried out its mission exceptionally well."

"Martha also performed exceptionally well. Martha displayed and identified each Russian and Chinese submarine tracking our fleet. It was so accurate that it could film the sailors on board the submarines it was tracking. Had this been a time of war, those subs would have been destroyed quickly. Martha has given us the ability to track and identify any hostile vessel on or below the surface of the ocean."

"What was amazing was that Martha not only tracked one Chinese submarine that was submerged underneath the hurricane but could see the movements of its crew on the boat even though it was under a hurricane."

The Rescue of the Nadia Marie

"The *Nadia Marie* incident which you are concerned about did have a security breach. Our CIA representative who was in Honolulu and upon hearing of the *Nadia Marie* decided to test the Martha system."

He had the Martha command center in Seneca, New York, run a check on the system. That check found the Schwartz family adrift on the ocean. The whole check took a matter of seconds.

"Our agent in Honolulu got together with his counterpart in Seneca and sent out the famous photo of the little girl, Nadia Marie Schwartz. To accomplish that they simply hacked into the Pentagon system and assigned the photo as having been sent from the White House Situation Room per the Office of the Joint Chiefs. How that message was sent in such a manner remains a secret to which only four people have knowledge of how it was done."

"A more serious breach did occur when the Seneca supervisor sent the photo to a childhood sweetheart in Des Moines, Iowa. I might add that there was no way to electronically trace that e-mail."

"A story has been leaked that the TV producer in Iowa, Sara Housely, had a Pentagon connection that had provided the photo from a military weather satellite."

"President Weedin took charge of the rescue operation and took responsibility for any messages originating from the situation room. That action eliminated any questions about where the messages originated."

"The two CIA agents involved in the leaks were disciplined for their actions. Agent Wilson, assigned to Honolulu, was transferred to our embassy in Ethiopia for his part."

"Director Stanford in charge of the Seneca operation was allowed to resign. President Weedin allowed Director Stanford to keep his top secret clearance."

"Both individuals justified their actions by claiming that their belief was that time was of the essence in rescuing the Schwartz family. They both felt that they had to take immediate action instead of waiting for the bureaucracy to respond. The president took that into account while making his decision. He felt that the motives of the two were commendable, but it was still a serious breach of security. The leaking of the satellite photo to an Iowa television station was too serious to ignore. Director Stanford was given the option of resigning with notice."

"President Weedin directed that no legal action be taken against the two."

"We were successful in convincing the Chinese MSS that a traitor had revealed the location of the *Wang Su*. A separate report on that operation is available for review if the director wishes to review it."

"Lastly, the Joint Chiefs were able to cover the costs of this extended operation by having funds transferred into Admiral Bender's CINCPAC budget from surplus research funds. Those funds are part of a CIA covert operations budget that is concealed within the Pentagon budget."

EPILOGUE

John Schwartz did not survive his ordeal. He died in a Honolulu hospital a few days after his rescue. Julie Schwartz survived. She never remarried. Her life was cut short by her experience and its effects on her body. On Christmas Eve, when Nadia was nineteen, Julie's body gave out.

Andrew "Andy" Wilson, the CIA agent in Honolulu was transferred to Ethiopia as punishment for his part in the breach of security of the Martha Satellite System. He was able to stop several terrorist attacks. Because of his devotion and loyalty to duty, he was promoted to the Middle East supervisor.

Before the end of his second term, President Weedin appointed Andy to the position of Deputy Chief of Operations at the CIA. Andy would eventually become the head of the CIA.

Richard Stanford, the Martha unit supervisor who leaked the photo of Nadia, was allowed to resign. He was immediately employed by the Rathdrum Corporation; the corporation that had designed and built the Martha Satellite. He would become the CEO of Rathdrum. He and his wife had one son named Sean.

Kai Che, the Chinese medic that had taken such good care of Nadia and her parents left the navy. People from all over the world donated money to a trust fund set up to pay for his college education. He became a pediatrician and wrote several children's books. His books were published worldwide in several languages. His nickname became "The Pirate."

Captain Chen Wei and his crew of the *Wang Su* returned to a hero's welcome. Chen Wei would be promoted to admiral. The Chinese Intelligence Agency, the MSS, took a less enthusiastic view. They wanted to know how the US Navy detected the *Wang Su*, a stealth sub, since another stealth sub in the area monitoring Task Force Tango was not detected.

Captain Chen Wei had anticipated the problem. He examined secret video installed in certain sections of his vessel. It was determined that on one shift, two of the three communications specialists were absent from their posts occasionally. Under intense questioning, the two admitted to having a sexual liaison. The third, a Lin Yun, admitted to knowing about the situation and remaining silent.

It was also found that the pair had sent clandestine and unauthorized personal messages to two more communications specialist assigned to a communications station located on an island in the Paracel Chain. All four were tried in secret and executed.

Lin Yun, the third communications specialist, was treated like an animal. He was thrown into solitary confinement. There was only a bucket of water and a bucket for relieving himself in his cell. Food was brought to him twice a day. No one was allowed to talk to him. His wife and family were treated as pariahs when it was learned that Lin was viewed as a traitor. Lin had been given the death penalty by a military tribunal. However, he was given one small glimmer of hope.

Lin Yun was allowed to appeal his sentence to the prime minister. Before the prime minister made a decision, the United States Ambassador to China arranged a spy swap with the prime minister. Lin Yun and his family were exchanged for a Chinese scientist serving a life sentence for espionage in the United States. Lin Yun and his family were subsequently relocated to Taiwan. He was never given an explanation for why the United States government rescued him from certain death or life in prison.

The Chinese MSS felt that Lin Yun was somehow involved in the *Wang Su* matter. There was no other explanation for why the United States arranged to take him in a spy swap for such a valuable agent.

Sheriff Eldon Fogus, the man who had started the rescue incident, was reelected for another term. When he retired, he took his dog and went fishing. He was found lying on the bank of a small lake still clutching his favorite fishing rod. At his memorial, his son stated that his father had finally been united with the wife he loved so much and found the peace he so desperately sought.

President Greg Weedin was elected to a second term in a landslide. Some pundits claimed that the people reelected him because he was viewed as the pirate chief who had saved a sad, forlorn little girl from certain death.

Nadia obtained a PhD degree in languages. She learned to speak and write seven languages fluently. After the rescue, Anna Hansen, the college student, became close friends with Nadia. When Nadia was out of school and ready to apply for a job, Anna got her a job with the US State Department as an interpreter. Within a short period, Nadia was recognized for her excellent work and became an interpreter for the president.

On a cold rainy night in Washington, DC, she collided with a young lawyer named Sean Stanford while they both were running for the same cab. Both of them shared the cab and an immediate friendship developed. They were married within a year. They had four children.

It was claimed by the family that when Richard Stanford was told who his son intended to marry, he was speechless. Richard never told his family about his part in Nadia's rescue when she was a child.

Over time, a strong bond developed between Nadia and her father-in-law. Richard Stanford and his wife Anna were killed in an automobile accident caused by a drunk driver. At his funeral, Nadia remarked that her father-in-law became the father she had lost so many years before.

www.ingramcontent.com/pod-product-compliance
Ingram Content Group UK Ltd.
Pitfield, Milton Keynes, MK11 3LW, UK
UKHW041954230426
12048UKWH00008B/327